F—k Boy 3

Nia Rich

F--k Boy

3

Nia Rich

Also by Nia Rich

Triangles

Never Going Back

My Love Is Deeper

Lovers Remorse

F—k Boy 3

Written by: Nia Rich
Copyright © 2019 Nia Rich

All rights reserved.

Cover: Tina Louise

This is a work of fiction. Names, characters, places are either the product of the authors imagination or are used fictitiously and any resemblance to actual persons, living or dead, business establishments, events, or locals, is entirely coincidental.

F--k Boy

3

Nia Rich

F—k Boy

Previously in F—k Boy......

Adara

I was sitting on the couch eating a mini bag of Cheetos. Ava was sitting on the couch next to me eating a bag of chips. Christmas was over, and the new year was approaching. The salon was booked solid for the next week, and it was my only day off. I spent the entire day relaxing. Wes called right when I stood up to walk to the kitchen.

When I answered, he said, "Adara."

"What?" I asked.

"I need to stop by right now. It's an emergency."

"What's wrong?"

"Some shit just went down at cuz's house and I need somewhere to be for a few hours. I got to come now Adara please."

I said, "Ok. Come on."

I hung up and took my cup of juice back to the couch. Wes rang my doorbell a few minutes later. I stood up and let him in.

"What's wrong?" I asked.

"Oh man. Cuz was having a little party. Some dumb ass dudes started fighting. We broke the fight up, and then one of them came back and started shooting, and then I bounced and called you. I just need somewhere to chill for a couple of hours until shit dies down."

"I am glad that you're ok Wes. Is your cousin ok?"

"Yes. Everybody is cool, but cuz said the cops is over there right now."

"Ok well. You can stay here. Me and Ava were about to go to bed soon. Do you need to stay the night?"

"I mean, if you don't mind. I'll be out of here in the morning."

"That is fine. I am just glad that you're ok."

Wes exhaled and said, "Me too."

"Anyways. How are you feeling?"

"I'm sleepy, but I am fine."

Wes looked at the bag of chips on the table. "You up in here eating chips?"

I laughed, "Yes. I just had a taste for them."

"You don't even like chips like that, so I know that's my baby that got you eating like that." he said.

I laughed again, and then I said, "Anyways. Do you want to help me put Ava to bed?"

"I got it you just chill." Wes said.

I watched him pick Ava up and walk with in his arms to her room. I thought about what Miles and Kyra said about giving it another chance, and then I went back to watching television.

***

"What the hell is all this stuff in my house?" I asked angrily.

Wes was sitting on the couch waiting for me to get home. I had just walked into my house from work and into a mess. There were boxes and shoes and clothes everywhere. When I left that morning, Wes asked me if he could chill because his cousin said his place was still hot. I knew that meant that cops were still creeping around his house. They were probably driving up and down the block or parked somewhere watching. I told him that he could chill at my place while I was at work, but I didn't say anything about him moving his stuff into my house.

"Adara I can explain." Wes said.

"Please do because I didn't tell you that you could move in."

"Earlier cuz called and told me to come and get some of my stuff because he had a bad feeling, so we packed up most of my stuff and put it in my car. When I got back here, cuz's girl called and said that the feds kicked in the door and took my cousin to jail. I put all my stuff in here because I don't have anywhere to put it right now"

I smacked my lips and said, "Wes."

"What? I apologize Adara. I didn't want to bother you at work."

"You couldn't go to your other baby mama's house?"

"Lesley lives with her mom, and I don't fuck with her like that."

I folded my arms, smacked my lips again, and groaned, "Wes.'

Adara, baby, listen. Let me chill here for a minute. I got money, I can help you with shit, and I won't be here for long."

I unfolded my arms, rubbed one of my hands across my forehead, and said, "Oh my God. Wes, I don't know."

"Plus, I can help you out with the Ava now that you are pregnant."

"Wes this is crazy."

"I know Adara. Can you do this for me please? I don't have anywhere else to go."

I took a deep breath, exhaled, and then I said, "Alright."

F—k Boy

F--k Boy

3

Nia Rich

Chapter 1

Adara

I pulled into to my driveway and parked my car. I looked around and saw a bunch of cars parked on the street in front of my house. I knew that meant that Wes had some of his friends over again. It was a Friday. I was tired I had been on my feet working all week and all that day, and I wasn't in the mood for company. I looked at my house. I could see that all the lights were on inside, and I could hear music and loud talking coming from the inside of my house.

I took a deep breath and rubbed my temples, and then I said, "Looks like daddy's got company again Ava."

I got out of the car, helped Ava out of her car seat, and then walked with her into the house. The strong scent of marijuana hit my nose when I walked in. Wes was at the table playing cards with three of his friends. I rolled my eyes when I saw them, and then I closed the door and locked it. His friends spoke to me, so I spoke back, and then I began removing me and Ava's coats.

Having friends over on Friday nights was becoming a regular occurrence for Wes and it was starting to get on my nerves. Plus, he had been living at my house way longer than I intended for him to be there, and he wasn't working again. I don't know how I ended up back in a relationship with Wes, but we were back together, living together, and our baby was due in a month and a half.

"Hey baby." Wes said as he stood up to greet me at the door.

"Hi." I said dryly.

Ava jumped into his arms, and said, "Daddy."

"Hey pretty girl." he said to her. He kissed her on the cheek, and then he kissed me on the lips.

I turned to walk towards my bedroom, so he followed me in there with Ava in his arms. I walked to my dresser, opened the top drawer, and pulled out pajamas for myself. I felt the baby moving inside of me, so I rubbed my stomach.

"Is the baby moving again baby?" he asked.

"Yea. He's been moving all day." I said.

"My son is a gangsta. He's just trying to let you know now before he comes out." he said.

I said, "Whatever."

"What's wrong baby?"

"Why are they here again?" I whispered.

"We're playing some cards baby."

"It smells like weed in here. I hope y'all weren't smoking weed in my house."

"Nah, we smoked outside."

"You didn't even tell me that you were having company. You could have given me a heads up."

"I'm sorry. I didn't know they were coming. They just stopped over for a minute."

"Wes, I just got home from work, I'm tired, and I don't feel like having company."

"Okay baby. Let me finish this game, and then I'll tell them they've got to go."

I rolled my eyes and said, "Fine. I hope you don't think this is going to keep going on. Especially after I have this baby."

"Don't be like that." he said.

"Whatever."

I took Ava out of his arms, put her on her feet, grabbed her hand and walked with her out of the bedroom towards the kitchen. He followed me out and, walked back to the table, and sat down to finish playing cards with his friends. I looked at the table and saw that everyone had beers including Wes. That added more irritation on top of how I was already feeling. Then, to top it all off, he hadn't been at work again all day, and hadn't so much as done the dishes, or taken the trash out.

I pulled a package of meat out of the sink. I had it thawing out all day while I was at work. I turned on the stove, seasoned the meat, put it in a pan, and then put the meat in oven. I started doing the dishes. I know Wes and his friends knew that I was irritated by the way I was slamming the dishes around.

After I was done, I walked back into the living room picked Ava up and took her with me into the bathroom. I needed to bath her and put her into her pajamas. I was cursing the day that I decided to have another baby by him. It was back to the same old shit again. He wasn't bringing in any money, in my house, eating up my damn food, drinking again, and running the streets again. Everything that I was afraid that was going to happen, and then some. Plus, my baby wasn't the only baby he had on the way. Leslie was about to have a baby by him too. She was due to have her baby any day.

Wes put on a good front in the beginning per usual. He was working, coming home every night, and helping out with Ava. Once I got six months into my pregnancy, things started going downhill. He got laid off from his job, and then slowly, the old him returned.

After I finished bathing Ava, I began putting her pajamas on. I knew that I wasn't going to get a chance to bathe until I put her to bed. Things would have been so much easier if Wes was helping me instead of drinking, smoking, and playing cards with his friends.

Wes walked into the room and said, "Baby, I'm about to get out of here. I'm about to go make a run with Black and them."

"When are you coming back?"

"I'll be right back. I promise."

"Wes, you've been running the streets again a lot for the past couple of months."

He exhaled, and then he said, "Adara don't start."

"Don't start what? I'm just saying. I'm not about to do this again with you during this pregnancy."

"I know baby. You're not."

"Ok then, when do you plan to stop, and when do you plan to get another job? I can't do this by myself. We're about to have two kids."

"Baby, I can't talk about that right now. I've got to go. We'll talk about it later."

He kissed me, kissed Ava, and then he rushed out of the door.

***

I woke up around three o'clock in the morning to use the bathroom. I noticed Wes wasn't home yet. I didn't know where he was, but I wasn't in the mood to call repeatedly, or search all around town trying to find him. My back and my stomach were aching, and I was feeling nauseated.

My second pregnancy was the worst. I was sick most of the pregnancy, I was always in pain or uncomfortable, and I had a few complications. I had a couple of miscarriage scares and for a while I wasn't sure if my baby was going to survive the pregnancy. My doctor told me that bed rest for the duration of my pregnancy was a strong possibility. The doctor didn't want me to go into premature labor and have the baby too early. I didn't want to be put on bed rest because I needed to work to keep money flowing. Especially with Wes not working again. All that was going on, and Wes was still doing what he wanted to do. I was too exhausted to put energy into where he was, but I was surely irritated that he wasn't home.

A few minutes after I laid back down in my bed, I heard Wes's car pull into the driveway. I quickly closed my eyes. I wanted him to think that I was asleep because I didn't want to be bothered. I heard his keys in the lock, and then I heard him open and close the door quietly. I listened to him make his way through the house without making a sound. I'm sure that he didn't want to disturb Ava while she was asleep. He probably didn't want to wake me up either because he didn't want to hear my mouth.

He crept into our bedroom and climbed right into the bed. He didn't take his clothes off or nothing. His clothes reeked of a mixture of cigarettes and marijuana smoke. He slid close to me and kissed me on my shoulder. I could smell alcohol on his breath. All the odors mixed together instantly irritated me and made me nauseas. I continued to lay there like I was asleep. I was praying that he would just pass out and leave me alone, but my prayers weren't answered. He proceeded to try and wake me up.

Wes whispered my name. I didn't respond, so he whispered it again, and then he lightly shook me. When I didn't say anything, he whispered my name a third time. I groaned, "Hmmmm?"

"You up?" he asked.

"You know I'm sleep. Why are you waking me up Wes?"

"You weren't sleep."

"Yes I was. Why are you waking me up at this time of morning?"

"Because I want to feel you."

"You're waking me up to have sex?"

"Yes."

"Wes, I'm not in the mood to have sex. I'm tired. I'm not feeling good, and I have to work in a few hours."

pulled me to him and said, "Don't make me beg baby."

"Stop Wes. I'm not in the mood and you stink. It's making me want to throw up."

"Adara it's been a long time."

"And you know why."

"I know, but baby I need you right now."

"I thought you said that you were coming right back?"

"I'm sorry baby. I was chilling with my people and the time got away from me."

"I asked you not to stay out late like this, but you do it anyway. You're starting this shit again." I said.

"Come on Adara, not tonight. I've already apologized. It won't happen again, ok? So, come here and give me a kiss."

"You've been drinking Wes."

"No I haven't."

"I can smell it."

"Ok. All I had is a beer."

"We're starting that shit again?"

"What shit?"

"Beer is alcohol Wes."

"Ok. I just had one."

"We both know that you had more than just one, and you shouldn't have had any. I thought you told me that you were done with drinking, but slowly I've been seeing you picking the habit back up, so when did that start?"

Wes sighed, and then he said, "Oh man. Don't start Adara. All I wanted to do is come home, make love to my woman, and pass out. I'm not trying to go through this right now."

"Not trying to go through what?"

"Fussing and arguing with you."

"Fusing and arguing? You want to know what I'm not trying to go through? Dealing with you drinking again and dealing with you being out all hours of the night doing only God knows what. I'm especially not trying to deal with you not working again. Speaking of that, you've been out of work for a month now Wes. When do you plan on getting another job?"

"Damn Adara. You really know how to kill a mood don't you. This pregnancy got you tripping."

"You up in here worried about a mood, and I'm worried about how we're going to take care of two kids and this household. Not to mention, you also have three other kids, and one on the way with your other baby's mother. I cannot be stressing. I'm trying to give birth to a healthy baby; your son, and this pregnancy has been complicated the entire time. You know that."

"I got us. We're gonna be fine." he said angrily.

"Nah Wes. I've heard that from you before. I'm not going through the same shit I went through when I was pregnant with Ava."

"Adara, I said I got this. I don't want to keep talking about this shit."

"Well, give me a reason not to talk about it then."

"You know what? You're really killing my fucking vibe with this bullshit."

I sat up in the bed and raised my voice, "Bullshit!? How me and your kids are going to live is bullshit Wes?" I'm talking about how we are going to keep food in this house and pay these bills. We have another mouth to feed. I can't do this on my own!"

"And I told you everything with be straight."

"Yea ok, and what's this having your friends over every weekend. I don't want those ruthless nobody's up in my house. You know that I don't like half of them."

"Oh ok. I see. You're gonna run down a list of shit you got a problem with tonight? I'm not in the mood for this shit. I came home to get some pussy and lay up next to you; not to argue!"

"I'm not thinking about sex! I want some fucking answers because I'm not going through this again Wes!"

"I'm not about to argue about this shit. I'm going in the living room to watch tv. Be quiet before you wake up Ava."

I paused with a frown on my face, and then I said, "Whatever."

Wes walked out of the room. I put my hand on my stomach, looked up at the ceiling and said, "Please tell me that I didn't make a mistake doing this again."

Chapter 2

Adara

"Hey sis! How are you?" Kyra said when I walked into the salon. She was standing at the front desk looking at the appointment book.

"I'm doing good. Thanks. How are you?" I asked.

"Oh, I've had better days." she said.

"Do you want to talk about it?"

"No but thank you." Kyra said. She turned to give me a hug, and then she touched my protruding belly.

"You're about ready to pop any day now, huh?"

"Girl just about. In another month and a half this will be over. I just hope he stays in there full term."

"I know. You had so many complications this pregnancy."

"I know, and the doctor keeps talking about putting me on bed rest. I don't want to be on bed rest. I have things to do."

"I hear you sis, but bed rest might be a good thing. It's important for you and the baby to be alright."

"I know."

"I hope that man of yours is not stressing you out."

"He's starting to, but I'm trying to not let little things get to me."

"Don't. You've got to bring a healthy baby into this world."

"You're right."

"Hey ladies!" Bianca said when she entered the salon.

"Hey girl!" I said. I was feeling nauseas again. I prayed that I could keep breakfast down.

"Hi sis!" Kyra said as she made her way to her station.

"Damn Adara. That belly is getting big girl." Bianca said.

"I know. I'm so over this pregnancy." I said.

"Girl, you're going to be done soon enough."

"Are you going to be able to hold down this salon when I have him?

"Of course, you know I've got you."

"Thanks girl." I said.

"No problem." she said, and then she turned to make her way to her station.

I looked at my watch. Nikita was going to be showing up any minute. She was my first appointment. I started setting up my station, and then I heard the door to the salon open. Nikita walked in. Her pregnant belly was as big as mine was. The look on her face told me that she was not in a good mood.

"What's wrong with you?" I asked.

She slammed her purse down on my station, and then plopped down in my chair.

"I think Jakari has been fucking some bitch in my house."

"What? Why do you think that?"

"Because I found an empty condom rapper in my trash."

I raised my eyebrows and said, "Whoa."

"Yea. He had the nerve to try to hide it underneath some stuff, but our son accidentally knocked the trash can over, and there it was clear as day."

"Why the hell would he throw it in the trash at home? Why didn't he just take it with him?"

"I don't know. The mutha fucka is slow as fuck and he is trifling. So, I called him after I dropped our son off at school to ask him about it, and he had the nerve to say that he doesn't know what I'm talking about."

"Girl, I've said this many times, I don't know why you stay dealing with his trifling, raggedy ass."

"I know. I'm so done with his ass."

"You always say that cousin, and then you stay."

"Um hum."

"But, you ain't no better than him now."

"How?"

"You're pregnant with another man's baby that Jakari thinks is his." I whispered.

"Karma." she said.

I chuckled, and then I said, "You better hope karma doesn't come back and bite you in the ass."

"Girl please. All the shit he put me through. I deserve to have this one little indiscretion under my belt."

I chuckled again and said, "Little? Ok. A pregnancy is not little cousin. Anyways, what are we doing to your hair?"

"Same old."

"Ok. We need to get you into a new hair style cousin. You've been rocking this for the last three years."

"I know. I'm ready for something new too, but I don't know what I want."

"I'll do some research and I'll come up with some options for you."

"Cool."

Bianca walked over to Nikita, "When are you due?"

"Soon."

"I know Jakari is going to be happy to have another son."

"He is." Nikita said, and then she looked at me.

I raised my eyebrows and gave her a smirk because I was the only person that knew that she wasn't having Jakari's baby.

"I got your invite for the baby shower. I will be there."

"Thank you." Nikita said.

After Bianca walked away, Nikita said, "Anyways, um have you talked to your sister Chanel lately?"

"No. I haven't heard from her in a while. Why?"

"Because I saw something online from one of those gossip sites about her husband."

I frowned and asked, "What?"

"That he was spotted with some female at a party. He was grabbing her butt and kissing her neck. Someone filmed it and posted it online."

"No." I said.

"Yup." Nikita said.

Bianca overheard Nikita and said, "Oh yea, I think that I saw that too. In the Shade Room, right?"

"Yup and they ran the story on TMZ." Nikita said.

"Oh no. That means it's going to go viral." I said.

"It already has cousin. Where have you been under a rock?" Nikita asked.

Kyra said, "I think I heard them talking about it on Dish Nation the other day. I was going to say something to you about it, but I forgot."

"Let me show you cousin." Nikita said.

She pulled her phone out of her purse, typed her code in to unlock the screen, clicked on to one of her social media pages, and scrolled through a few pages until she found the video. She handed me her phone. I took her phone and watched the video. Bianca and Kyra walked over to watch the video with me. There Orlando was grabbing on some girls fake booty and kissing her on the neck at a party somewhere. I felt anger shoot through my entire body.

"This mother fucker." I said angrily as I handed Nikita her phone.

"Girl." Nikita said.

"That's a damn shame." Bianca said. She shook her head and turned to walk away.

"That is horrible. I know your sister must feel terrible."

'I'm not surprised. I told her that she shouldn't marry his raggedy ass. I can't believe that I didn't hear about this. I've got to call her." I said.

Nikita said, "I think you should. They are alleging that he is cheating on her with this girl."

The three of them continued to tell me all the details around the news stories, blogs, and comments from fans and spectators. I was listening, but I couldn't keep my mind off the sharp pains that I was feeling in my stomach. I quickly did Nikita's hair, did another client, cleaned up the shop a little, and then went to use the bathroom. Panic rushed through my body when I saw blood in my panties.

"Oh fuck." I said as I flushed the toilet. I washed my hands, rushed out of the bathroom, and called my doctor's office. They told me to come in right away, so I grabbed my purse and keys, and headed out of the salon.

"Ladies, I've got to go the doctor."

"Are you ok cousin?" Nikita asked.

"Um, I don't know."

"Do you want me to come with you?" Nikita asked.

"Could you?"

"Yep. I got you cousin."

"Bianca can you do Lisa when she comes in? She was my last client. I'm sure she won't mind."

"Yup. I got her."

"Ok. I'll text her and let her know."

"Let us know what the doctor says." Kyra said.

"I will text y'all." I said as I was walking out of the door.

I called Wes as we were walking out of the door, but he didn't answer per usual. I sent him a text message telling him that I was heading to the hospital.

Something is wrong. Heading to the hospital, Call asap.

Nikita and I made it there in no time. I called Wes a few more times, but no answer. I put my phone away and tried my hardest not to get frustrated because I didn't want to add to the stress that I was already feeling. Nikita sat there with me while the doctor checked me and ran a few tests, and then she told me what I didn't want to hear. That I was being put on bed rest for the duration of my pregnancy. I was frustrated and Wes was nowhere to be found.

I left the hospital feeling aggravated. I didn't want to be put on bed rest. I needed to keep working, and I couldn't count on Wes to be at home with me daily helping me with Ava. He didn't even call me back that day until I was already home. He gave me some lame ass excuse for the reason that he was unreachable. I wasn't in the mood to address him about where he was. I had other things to worry about, and I couldn't keep my mind off my sister Chanel and what I had heard about her husband Orlando. I made a mental note to call her and check on her as soon as possible.

Chapter 3

Chanel

"Why do you keep lying to me Orlando! It's all over social media! Look at this! Who is this girl that you're kissing on!" I yelled.

"Look, I already told you that I wasn't kissing on her."

"I'm watching you do it in this video! You're going to keep up with the lies!? First, it wasn't you in the video! Now, it's you weren't kissing her?!"

"I was whispering something in her ear."

"Whispering something in her ear? Did you need to grab her ass to do that!?"

"I was drunk and I'm not going to keep talking about this! The shit happened! That's that!"

"That's that!? That's all you've got to say!? I can't believe you! You've embarrassed me in front of the entire world! My family has seen this video! Your family has seen this video! All you've got say is that's that!?"

"I just told you that I'm not going to keep talking about this shit!"

"Fuck you alright!"

Whap!

Orlando smacked me hard, and then he grabbed my neck, pulled me to him, and yelled, "Shut the fuck up! I don't give a fuck how mad you think you are. You're not about to keep talking to me crazy! Like I said, it is what it is! There ain't shit that you can do about it at this point! Leave me the fuck alone! What the fuck you gonna do? Leave? Leave then! Where the fuck are you going to go? Huh? You ain't got shit! Don't nobody give a fuck about you!"

He threw me to the floor and walked off. I curled up in a ball on the floor and sobbed hard. I heard him walk out of the door, get into his car, and leave. I laid there for a while and cried, and then I gathered myself, picked myself up off the floor, and walked to our bedroom to lie down. I just wanted to sleep it all away. I looked in my bedroom mirror and touched my new bruise by my mouth. It was swollen and red, but it had not turned black yet.

"How the hell did it come to this?" I asked myself.

I dug around in my drawer to find a bottle of prescription Percocet's I had gotten from my dentist the last time I had work done on my teeth. I picked up a glass of water I had on the dresser and swallowed one of the pills, and then I laid down in my bed to let the medication take me out of the misery that I was feeling.

***

I woke up several hours later to a phone call from Adara. Orlando still wasn't home. It wasn't late night, but it was the time a husband should be home with his wife. At first, I wasn't going to answer the phone because I didn't feel like talking. I didn't feel like talking to anyone. I was embarrassed about the video and I didn't want to talk about it or answer any questions. My family had been calling me for days trying to find out what happened or give their opinion about what I should do. It was already bad enough that my mother had called me to give her brutally honest thoughts about Orlando, but I had countless cousins and aunties calling me too. Some I hadn't talked to in years and some that I didn't really know.

Everyone was trying to get in on what was going on in my life. All because Orlando being stupid on a drunk night.

At that point in our marriage, I didn't know if Orlando was cheating on me, or if he was just flirting with women while he was out with his friends. Either way his actions were nothing that a husband should've been doing when he had a wife at home.

I listened to the phone ring again, and then I decided to answer the phone because I hadn't talked to Adara in a while. I reached over to my nightstand, picked up my phone, and swiped the screen to answer it.

"Hello." I said. My voice was low and groggy. My head was still under my blanket.

"Hey sis. How are you?" Adara asked.

"I'm fine sis. How are you?"

"I'm good, but are you sure that you are ok? Because you don't sound it.?"

"I'm fine sis. I just woke up."

"Well, I was just calling to check up on you. I saw that bullshit with Orlando. What the hell was that about?"

"It was nothing Sis."

"Nothing? It looked like a whole lot of something to me."

"It was a misunderstanding."

"Sis, are you serious? He was kissing on another woman. How is that a misunderstanding?"

"He wasn't kissing her. He was whispering something to her."

"Is that what he told you or is that what you saw? Because I watched the video and he was clearly kissing on the woman."

"It was dark, and the video was kind of grainy."

"Are you really making up excuses for his punk ass?"

"Look, sis. It's not a big deal, and I don't want to talk about it anymore."

"Not a big deal? Chanel, do you hear yourself? Who are you? That dirty bastard has always been a bitch ass, fuck boy. He has always done dirt, and he still is while married to you. I told you that you were making a mistake marrying him."

"I don't want to talk about this right now sis. I've got to go."

"Sis. Look, I apologize. I just wanted to check on you and make sure that you were ok."

"I'll call you later. I need to fix dinner and clean the house before Orlando gets home."

"Ok sis. Take care of yourself and don't forget to call me. I love you."

"I won't sis. I love you too."

I hung up, pulled the blanket off my head, and sat up in my bed. I was still feeling a little dizzy from the pain killer that I took earlier. I looked around my dark room and realized how alone I felt in Orlando's big house. He was never home and the days he was home it was almost like he wasn't there because he barely talked to me. He was either talking on his phone, sending text messages, or scrolling through his social media pages.

I swung my feet over the side of the bed, and then I clicked on my lamp. I took a deep breath and slid out of our King size bed. I didn't feel like getting out of bed, but I knew if I didn't cook dinner Orlando would be mad. Even if he didn't eat it that night, he would still be mad that I didn't cook. I clicked the hallway light on and made my way down the stairs to the kitchen. I was moving slow and I wished that I was still sleep. When I walked past the large mirror on the wall in the hallway, I got a quick glimpse at the bruise by my mouth that Orlando put there earlier. I paused, looked at it, and then I turned away from the mirror and walked into the kitchen.

I pulled out everything I needed to make my husband a meal. There was a new recipe I got from a cooking show that I planned to try. I hoped that he would like it. Even though he had completely disrespected me earlier that day, I still wanted to do something for him that would make him happy. I went to work on the meal for my husband. It took me about an hour and a half to finish cooking the food, then I set our table.

I was standing in the kitchen taking a bottle of wine out of the wine holder to put it in a bucket of ice when Orlando walked in. He walked in looking at his phone. He walked past me as if I weren't there. He didn't speak, nor did he look at me. He walked through the kitchen, into the living room, and sat down on the couch. He never took his eyes off his phone. I picked up the bottle of wine and the bucket of ice. I walked with it over to the table, and then I put it down. I was irritated with the way Orlando ignored me, but I took a deep breath, and then I slowly walked to the living room. I stood there in silence for a moment to see if he would acknowledge my presence, but he didn't. He continued to ignore me, so I finally said something to him.

"So you're not going to say anything to me?"

He was silent.

"Orlando."

"What? I'm busy."

"Too busy to speak to your wife?"

He was silent again. I stood there for a few seconds, and then I said, "I cooked dinner. You should come and eat."

He stood up, walked towards me, and then he said, "I'm not hungry. I already ate."

He walked past me and disappeared to the other side of the house. I was so frustrated I couldn't even speak. I just cleared the table, put the meal that I cooked away, and sat on the couch in my thoughts.

Chapter 4

Chanel

"Are you losing weight girl? You look smaller." Lisa asked when she answered the door to let me into her home.

"Do I?" I asked as I walked into her home.

"Yes."

"It's not intentional." I said.

"Well, you look good girl." Lisa said, and then she reached out to hug me.

I hugged her, and then I said, "Thank you."

"Oooo look at you; looking all skinny." Letisha said when I walked into the living room where the other wives were hanging out. Letisha had her box braids pulled into a bun. She was looking a little heavier than normal, but I didn't mention it.

"That is what Lisa just said." I said.

"Doesn't she?" Lisa asked. She had her natural, sandy brown, curly hair straightened with blonde highlights. It hung past her shoulders.

"Yes you do." Tami said. Tami had her hair pulled back into a jet-black twenty-inch ponytail.

I gave Letisha and Tami a hug, and then I sat down on the couch next to Letisha. Until they said something about my weight, I hadn't realized that I had lost so much. I hadn't seen the wives in a while. I had completely drawn back from talking to people and hanging out since Orlando's alleged affair with another woman was all over the celebrity gossip news, blogs, and social media. I didn't want to talk to or see anybody, and Orlando was treating like I was the one who cheated. He was still being mean as ever, distant, and the one time that I did try to go out, he threw a fit. Talking about he didn't want me around Lisa and Letisha's gossiping ass's. He ripped my dress off me that day after smacking me. I locked myself in the bathroom and cried for about an hour.

Since that day, the only thing that I could think of was when was I going to get my husband back. When was he going to be nice to me again, and when was I going to see the man I fell in love with and married again? When was Orlando King going to show back up? Because the man that was in my house was a stranger.

"How was Miami Kamira?" Letisha asked.

Kamira looked up from her phone. I noticed her long coffin shaped nails were blinging with all kinds of rhinestones and jewels on them.

She said, "Me and my husband had a blast. We need to take a girls trip down there. The wives down there are really cool."

"We should do that. I'm in need of a vacation." Tami said.

"Me too." Lisa said.

The small talk was cool, but it was a cover up. The energy in the room was off. I knew the elephant in the room was me and my situation. Everyone wanted to know about it, but no one wanted to be the one to bring it up or ask me. Part of me hoped that no one would bring it up, but Letisha being the kind of woman she was could not hold her tongue. I knew it was coming by the way she looked at her best friend Lisa before she spoke.

"So, what's been up with you since Orlando was all on the blogs with that hoe?" Letisha asked.

"Letisha." Tami said.

Kamira's raised her eyebrows, and then looked up from her phone.

"What? Y'all were thinking it. I just said it." Letisha said.

"You don't have to answer that." Lisa said.

"No it's ok." I said.

"He lied about it didn't he? He said that he didn't do it, huh?" Letisha asked.

Kamira's eyebrows were still raised. Tami and Lisa were silent waiting for my answer.

I instantly felt uncomfortable, but I was trying hard not to let it show. I cracked my knuckles, and then I said, "He did. He said that he wasn't kissing her in the video. After he told me that it wasn't him in the video."

"Ah hell nah." Letisha said.

"Man." Tami said as she was shaking her head.

"That's messed up." Kamira said.

"That is normal Orlando shit." Letisha said.

"That was clearly him in the video." Lisa said.

"I know. I was livid. I pressed him for the truth, but he wouldn't fess up. He claimed that he was whispering in her ear."

"Oh my gosh. That's a fucking lie." Letisha said.

"I mean the video was kind of grainy so you really can't tell." I said.

"Girl please. You can see it clearly. He is kissing that woman. Don't let him manipulate you into believing that lie." Letisha said.

Lisa cut into Letisha oncoming rant and said, "Um, I'm sorry that happened. I know how you feel. Let us know if you need anything, ok."

"Yea girl that is messed up. I'm here if you need me." Tami said.

"Me too." Kamira said.

Letisha said, "I'm sorry y'all. It just pissed me off when I saw it. True Orlando bullshit. I was ready to fight him for you girl. Excuse me if I'm saying too much."

"Oh it's ok." I said as I held back tears.

"You let me know if you need anything as well. Especially if you want to jump him or something. I'm with it." Letisha said.

"Girl stop." Lisa said.

"What? I want to whoop his ass." Letisha said.

I stood up and excused myself to the bathroom. I didn't want them to see me cry. I quickly walked to the bathroom, closed and locked the door, and sat down on the tub. I took a deep breath, and then let my tears flow. I pulled some tissue from the roll tissue roll to dab my face.

A few minutes later, I heard a knock at the door, and then I heard Lisa's voice.

"Are you ok?" she asked.

"Yes." I responded.

"Can I come in?" she asked.

I stood up, unlocked and opened the door. She looked at me, walked in, and closed the door behind her. She hugged me and let me cry into her shoulder.

"I'm sorry." she whispered.

I nodded my head and continued to cry for a little while, and then I said, "Thank you."

"Girl, It's cool. I got you. I know how it is."

"It's just embarrassing you know?" I responded.

"I know. Trust me. My husband is not perfect. I've been right where you are before. Letisha can be a little harsh, but she doesn't mean anything by it. That's just how she is. She means well though."

"I know. I just wasn't ready to talk about it."

"I understand. Are you going to be ok?"

"Yea."

"I know you're hurt and it's rough right now, but eventually it will get better, and if it doesn't, you can always leave. Choose yourself. The lifestyle isn't always worth the pain."

"I hear you."

"Plus, we're friends now, and my friendships are for life, so we'll just find you a new man. One better looking than Orlando thinks he is." Lisa said.

I giggled a little through my sniffles. She chuckled with me, and then she said, "I'm here if you need me. For anything, ok?"

"Ok." I said, and then I dabbed the tears in my eyes with the wet tissue I had in my hand.

Lisa hugged me, and then she said, "I'll let you clean up. When you rejoin us, I'll make some drinks? You need it. Is that cool?"

"Yes. Thank you, Lisa."

"No problem." she said, and then she quietly left the bathroom.

I looked at myself in the mirror. In the year that I had been married to Orlando, I had slowly sunken into a new me. A me that I didn't know. My reflection had shown that I had lost a considerable amount of weight. I was starting to develop dark circles under my eyes in addition to the bruises I had in various places on my body. I had also picked up a pill addiction to cope. I didn't know myself.

I adjusted the short pixie style haircut that I got for Orlando. The haircut that he didn't care anything about. I dried the tears from my eyes, fixed my make-up, and then I left the bathroom and rejoined the wives in the living room. Lisa told us to follow her to her kitchen so she could make us drinks.

As we were walking into the kitchen, Kamira asked, "Is that a bruise on your arm girl?"

I had totally forgot about that bruise. Orlando had put it there the other night during one of his angry fits because I did something that he didn't like. He had punched me in the arm and pushed me into the bathroom door.

I said, "Oh, girl I was cleaning. I tripped and fell into the door and hit my arm on the doorknob."

"Oh wow. It looks like it hurts." Kamira said

"Not anymore. I actually forgot it was there." I said. I ignored the look Letisha gave Lisa and changed the subject.

I said, "So, when are we planning this Miami trip?"

"I'll get everything together and let all of you know when it is." Lisa said as she handed everyone a glass.

"I can't wait. This should be fun! I'm in need of a vacation away from my kids." Letisha said.

"I haven't been to Miami in years." Lisa said. "It should be fun to visit with the wives down there."

"Did you hear that what's his name wife is divorcing him and tryna take more than half down there in Miami?" Letisha asked.

"Yea I heard about that." Kamira said.

There she was gossiping again. I was happy that it wasn't about me. I sat back and listened to the wives chat about other people and enjoyed my drink and the peace away from Orlando.

Chapter 5

Kyra

Kyra checked on the food in her slow cooker, and then she began cleaning the dishes she used to prepare the meal that she was cooking. She stopped to look in the mirror and adjusted her light brown naturally curly hair. Her caramel skin was oiled and smelling sweet. Her make-up was natural looking which made her shiny red lipstick pop. She smiled at her reflection as she adjusted the dress she was wearing. She heard keys in the lock of her door. Kyra knew that it was her live-in boyfriend returning home from working on the road for the past couple of months.

She was happy that he was home, so she ran to the door and jumped in his arms when he opened it.

"Hey baby!" she exclaimed as she wrapped her legs and arms around him.

"Hey boo." Corey said, as he held her in his arms and hugged her.

"You look good baby and you smell good."

"Thank you. You do too." she said as he stared at her and rubbed his hands into her naturally curly hair.

"I missed you." she said.

"I missed you more baby." he said, and then he kissed her.

Corey kicked the door closed as they kissed, and then he walked with her in his arms to their bedroom. He laid her on the bed and began kissing her slowly and gently down her body. When he reached her waist, he pushed her floor length dress up, pulled her panties off, and began kissing her lower lips. Kyra moaned when she felt his lips on her peach and his tongue on her pearl.

"I missed this pussy." he said.

"She missed you." Kyra moaned.

Corey continued to caress her pearl with his tongue. Kyra grabbed his head and moaned everything she'd wanted to say to him for the months that he was gone. She missed her man and needed what he was giving her badly. She rode his tongue strokes until she reached her peak. Her body froze as she screeched a few high notes to the ceiling.

When he felt her relax, he stood up and began undressing. Once he was naked, he removed the rest of her clothing, pushed one of her legs up, and pushed his love inside of her. She moaned sounds of passion when she felt her man inside of her. She hadn't seen him in months, and she was anticipating his arrival. She needed to feel his touch, smell his scent, kiss his lips, and feel him inside of her.

Kyra wrapped her arms around his neck and pulled him down to her. He placed his lips on hers and began kissing her passionately as he thrust inside of her. She stopped kissing him just in time to let out loud moans when she released onto him. When he felt her, he grabbed the headboard and thrust harder. She gently dug her nails into his back as he began pounding faster. He leaned down to kiss her again before telling her that he loved her, and then he lost himself and pulled out. He grunted loudly as he let himself go onto her stomach.

"Shit baby. I needed that." he said between breaths.

"I know me too. Facetime sex wasn't doing it this time." Kyra said.

"I know. I couldn't wait to get back here to you."

"I couldn't wait either."

Corey kissed her, and then he said, "Don't move. Let me go and get you a towel."

He climbed out of bed, walked to their bathroom, grabbed a washcloth out of the cabinet, and walked to the sink. He wet the rag and then walked back into the bedroom. He cleaned the mess he left on Kyra's stomach, and then he walked back into the bathroom so he could clean himself. When he was finished, he climbed back into the bed next to his woman and pulled her into his arms.

***

Kyra opened her eyes and looked at her man lying next to her asleep. She stared at his face for a few minutes. They'd both passed out after sex and fell into an orgasm induced coma. She didn't even know that they had fallen asleep until she woke up. She picked up her phone from the nightstand and looked at the time. They'd been asleep for a couple of hours. She put her phone back on the nightstand and looked back at her man. She smiled at how peaceful he looked lying next her. Kyra looked at his eyes, his nose, his salmon colored lips, and then she looked at his muscular chest, abs, and arms. She loved the shoulder tattoo sleeve he had. It was a tribal design that they picked out together. She wondered at times how she ended up with a man like Corey.

She never in a million years thought she would end up in a relationship with a former drug dealer turned DJ; a white man at that. She always planned to marry and have a bunch of kids by one of those woke type of brotha's. One of those hotep, five percent, Muslim type of brotha's who prayed five times a day, called his woman queen, and lived a vegan lifestyle. Kyra's mother and father were both Muslims and would roll over in their graves if they saw the man she was in love with.

Kyra lost both her parents right after her eighteenth birthday to a fatal car accident and she missed them every day. Life without them was something that she had to come to terms with and it didn't happen overnight. She lost herself for a little while after she lost them.

After her parents died, everything in her life changed. She started partying a lot, drinking too much, and not caring much about her life. She met Corey in the middle of that phase. After an almost fatal night driving while drunk, she decided that she needed to take control of her life again and figure out life without her parents.

She put herself through college, got her degree, and then decided to try beauty school. She'd always liked doing hair; especially for her mom and friends, but she had never thought she would be a stylist. She did hair for fun. Turning it into a career was not her plan. Her mom always encouraged her to go to beauty school, but she had other plans for her life. She was going to finish school, find a job in a large company, so she could climb the corporate ladder, and become a manager of some department. She decided that she would make her mom happy and fulfill her mom's dream of her becoming a stylist. She figured she could give her mom in death what she didn't get a chance to give her in life.

Kyra smiled at Corey as she watched him sleeping. She could've laid there with him all day, but she knew that she needed to get dinner finished and get herself prepared for work at the salon in the morning. She had back to back clients all the next day, and she knew that she needed all the energy that she could get to make it through the day.

Kyra slid out of bed, put on her robe and slippers, and walked out of the bedroom. She walked into the kitchen and pulled the top off the slow cooker and looked at the meat inside of it. She would have pulled a piece out to taste it, but she was raised vegan and only cooked meat for her man. She could tell by the look and smell that it was almost done and just the way he liked it. She put the cover back on the pot, pulled a lighter out of the kitchen drawer, grabbed a package of incense, and lit a few of them. She walked through her house placing them in incense holders, and then she lit her candles that were placed in different areas of her house. After she was finished, she walked back to the kitchen to make her part of the dinner which consisted of organic vegetables and tofu. A few minutes after she got started, she heard the bedroom door creep open, and then the sound of footsteps coming towards her. She knew that meant Corey had woken up and probably smelled the food cooking.

Corey walked into the kitchen shirtless with a pair of flannel pajama pants on and house shoes. He scratched his head, sniffled, and then he said, "Smells good in here baby."

Kyra smiled and said, "Thank you."

He walked over to the pot, pulled the cover off, and asked, "What's in here?"

"You already know." she said.

"Ahh my favorite." he said before sniffling again.

"Yep." Kyra said as she continued to sauté her vegetables and tofu in the pot on the stove.

"See that's why I love you." he said.

Corey sniffled and then he walked over to Kyra and hugged her from behind. Kyra smiled when she felt her man's body up against hers. She loved when he hugged her from behind. Corey kissed her shoulder, and then she turned around, wrapped her arms around his neck, and looked him in the eyes.

She said, "I missed you."

"I missed you too." he said. He kissed her, and then he sniffled again.

Kyra stared into his eyes and then asked, "What's wrong with you? Are you coming down with something?"

He sniffled again, and said, "Yea baby. I think I'm coming down with a cold or something."

She was silent for a moment, and then she said, "Corey."

"What?"

"You're not lying to me, are you?"

"Lying about what?"

"I hope we're not about to go through this again?"

"Go through what baby?"

"You know what."

Corey sucked his teeth, moved her hands from around his neck, stepped back, and said, "Come on Kyra. Don't start."

Kyra folded her arms, and asked, "Don't start what?"

"Questioning me like I'm a child."

"Corey, you know every time you go out on the road, you come back with a habit."

"Kyra. I'm coming down with something, ok. End of discussion."

"I hope so. Because you left here clean. I hope you did not go back out on the road and pick up your habit again."

"Here you go tripping. I said, I'm fine. Chill out."

"I'm not doing this again Corey."

"Not doing what?" Corey asked angrily.

"I'm not dealing with your drug addiction again. You just finally got clean before you left, and you promised me that you were done with that mess. I do not want to go down that road again. The late nights, your disappearing some days and I can't find you. Your spending all of our money. You're coming home high and drunk from the club acting crazy and talking crazy. I can't do it. I told you that before you left."

"Look, Kyra, we don't need to talk about this. I said, I'm fine. Ok? I just got home. Don't ruin our good night. Now, can we eat?"

Kyra stared into his eyes for a moment before she said, "Ok. Corey."

She took a couple of plates out of the dishwasher and began filling them with food. Kyra handed Corey his plate and picked up her plate. He followed her to the dining room table and they both sat down to eat.

Chapter 6

Adara

I gave birth to my son early. Eight weeks too early to be exact. My doctor tried hard to stop me from delivering early, but my son just didn't want to stay in my belly full term. He made his way into this world at 32 weeks. He was only weighing a little over three pounds. My doctor told me that they were going to keep him in the NICU until he was strong enough to eat and breathe on his own. My doctor told me that it could be up to a month before my baby would be released from the hospital to go home.

With all that going on, the only two people at the hospital with me were my mom and my cousin Nikita. Wes was nowhere to be found. I had called him repeatedly on the way to the hospital and while I was in labor. Nothing from him. His phone kept going to voicemail. I was extremely irritated, but I had to focus on what was going on with my body and my baby. I sent him a bunch of text messages, and then I gave my phone to my mom and told her to answer it when he called.

He finally called after my son was born, and then he showed up at the hospital. He had the nerve to walk into my hospital room high and drunk. He reeked of the smell of weed and alcohol. I smelled it when he hugged me. I gave him a hard stare, and then I rolled my eyes.

"I've been calling you like crazy Wes. Where have you been?" I asked angrily

"I'm sorry baby. I was hitting stings with my boy and my phone died. You know that I wanted to be here."

"But you weren't." I shot back.

"Baby, I wanted to be here. I'm mad that I missed the birth of my son. I apologize baby. I really do. I'm here now, ok?"

"Whatever Wes." I said with a roll of my eyes.

I folded my arms over my chest and rolled my eyes again, and then he asked, "Where is he?"

"He is in the NICU. He was born too early, and he may be in there a while."

"Damn. Really?"

"Yes."

"How early?"

"About 2 months. He was only three pounds."

"Oh man baby. Is he going to be ok?"

"The doctor said that they will keep him until he can eat and breathe on his own. Until then, we have our fingers crossed that he is strong."

"Wow. I'm sorry baby." he said with sadness in his eyes.

He leaned down to hug me, and then he kissed me on the cheek. The smell of weed and alcohol made me nauseous, but I really didn't have the energy to address it. I didn't return the affection, and when he lifted up to look at me, I gave him a look that said that I was pissed.

"Baby I know you're mad-"

I cut him off and said, "Wes, I don't even have the energy right now."

My mom stood up and walked over to Wes and said, "Hey sweetie."

Her turned to hug her and replied, "Hey ma."

"I'm glad you could make it. I almost thought you weren't going to come. I was getting worried about you." she said.

"I apologize that I made it late. I didn't mean to ma. I swear I didn't mean to. I really wanted to be here." Wes replied.

"It's ok. Congratulations." she said.

"Thank you." he said.

"Walk with me, so I can take you to go and see your son."

"Ok ma. Thank you."

"No problem. Come on." she said, and then she turned to me and said, "We'll be right back baby." She kissed me on the forehead and walked out of the room with Wes.

Nikita put her phone down and asked, "Girl are you, ok?"

"No, I'm not. I wanted to smack the shit out of him."

"I know you did."

"Girl, and then he had the nerve to come up in here smelling like weed and alcohol. I know you smelled him."

"Nah, but he looked high as fuck though girl."

"Ugh. I can't believe he came in here like that; knowing that my mom is here."

"I hear you."

"When he hugged me, I could smell it all on him, so I'm sure my mom could smell it when she hugged him." I said. I put my hand on my forehead and shook my head.

"She probably did." Nikita said.

"How is the father of my children not going to be here for birth of his child because he was out running the streets doing whatever? Uuugh, I'm so irritated girl."

Nikita said, "Don't stress about it girl. You got other things to worry about. We need to pray that your son will be ok, so he can go home."

"You're right girl. Let me calm down."

"Please will you cousin. At least for me and your son."

"Ok. I got you cousin. Thank you."

"Always." she said, and then she stood up and asked if I needed anything.

I said, "No girl. I'm ok."

"Alright, I'm going to step out for a second to call Jakari back."

"Ok."

After Nikita walked out, I sat there for a few minutes in my thoughts. I was so irritated with Wes that I wasn't able to process the fact that I had just had a premature baby who was in the intensive care unit.

I closed my eyes, exhaled, opened my eyes, took a few breaths to calm down, and then I closed my eyes again and said a prayer for me and my baby.

"God please give me and my son strength. Amen."

When I opened my eyes, Wes and my mother were walking back into my hospital room. Wes walked over to grab a chair and carry over to the side of my bed. My mother went to where she was sitting and started to gather her things.

"He is little, but he looks good daughter. He is actually Wes's twin."

"Yes he is a mini me. I'm so happy to see him. I can't wait until I can hold him."

"Yes I hope he gets strong soon." she said, and then she walked up to my bed and said, "Daughter I am going to go and get some rest, but I will be back up here tomorrow to visit you and my grandson."

"Ok."

"Y'all good?"

"Yes." I said.

"Ok. Congrats again to the both of you. Play nice." she said.

My mom hugged and kissed the both of us, and then she walked out of the door. Nikita was walking in as my mom was walking out, so she stopped to give Nikita a hug before leaving out.

"Hey cousin. I got to get out of here, but I will call you to check on you later ok." Nikita said when she entered the room.

"Yes. Thank you for being here." I said.

"Girl you know I wouldn't miss it for anything. Plus, I'm next and I'm going to need all the support I can get. I never planned to be doing this a second time."

I chuckled a little and said, "You know I got you."

"Congrats again you two. Bye Wes."

She left, and then it was just me and Wes. I put my focus on the television to avoid looking at him. I was still fuming about him showing up to the hospital late.

He cleared his throat and said, "I know that you're mad at me babe."

"You're damn right I'm mad Wesley." I said without looking at him.

"You're calling me by my full name now?"

I was silent. I kept my eyes on the television.

"Can you forgive me?" he asked.

"You missed the birth of your son."

"Not on purpose."

"Doesn't matter. You were supposed to be here."

"I wanted to be here."

"But you weren't."

"I was getting money for us."

I looked at him and said, "Getting money Wes? You're back on that again? What happened to finding another job? We have two kids now, not to mention your three other kids and the one that is on the way."

"I'm doing what I got to do."

"Doing what you got to do would be getting out here and getting a real job, so you can take care of your kids."

"Come on now. Why are you going there? I am taking care of my business Adara, so you don't need to worry about that. As long as you and the *kids* that *I* have with *you* are taking care of, that's all you need to worry about."

"Drug money is not about to do that."

"I'm not about to talk to you about this in this hospital. Like I said, I apologize for not being here for the birth of my son, but I'm here now, ok?"

I rolled my eyes and looked back at the television. He stood up and sat on my bed.

"Don't look away from me."

"I am looking away from you Wes because you need to get it together."

"I am getting it together."

"How Wesley? You're back in these streets. You're hanging with these dudes you know don't have your best interest in mind. You're drinking again. You're staying out all hours of the night again. You came up in here late; smelling like weed and liquor; knowing my mother was here. You missed the birth of your son. The baby you begged me to keep, and you're telling me that you want me to be ok with all of this?" I folded my arms again and looked him directly in his eyes.

He exhaled, and then he said, "Adara, Thanks for bringing our baby into this world. I know you're stressed right now because he's a preemie, but everything going to be ok."

"Did you ever think that I had him early because I've been stressing? Stressing about you. I was up all night looking for you last night. You came walking up in the house after four o'clock in the morning. We got into, and then you walked out. Went back out there to wherever it was you came from. You had the nerve to turn your phone off when I was trying to call you, and my water broke two hours later while I was sitting up in bed pissed off at you."

"I'm sorry about last night baby. I just didn't want to hear you bitching and complaining, when I'm trying to make a way for us."

"Ok, but I've been calling you all day. I know at some point you turned your phone back on."

"I did babe, but honestly, my phone was dying when I left the house last night. After I turned it back on, I never put it on a charger, so it died. I didn't have my charger with me. I left it at the house with you because I forgot to grab it. None of my homeboys got an IPhone, so no one had a charger, and then I got carried away with what I was doing. When I got to a charger, I turned my phone back on and got all your messages about the baby coming, so I came straight here."

"Great explanation Wesley."

"I don't have to lie baby. My phone is dead now. I didn't even have time to charge it up good before coming here. Look."

He took his phone out of his pocket and showed it to me. He pressed the power button and it wouldn't boot up. I pushed the phone away from my face.

"Don't you think I would have been calling my mom and family right now to let them know that you had the baby?"

"Whatever."

"Alright then, now will you forgive me please?"

"Um hum."

"Alright. We'll deal with everything else later. We have to deal with our son right now. I love you."

"I love you too."

He kissed me on my lips, and then he stood up and asked, "Where's a plug, so I can plug this phone up?"

"Over there."

Wes stood up, and then the doctor knocked at the door and walked in. She introduced herself to Wes, and then began to examine me. I was still upset, but I pushed it into the back of my mind so I could focus on me and my new baby boy.

Chapter 7

Chanel

The smell of bacon cooking woke me up. I slowly opened my eyes, and then I sat up in the bed. I looked next to me. There was a large white box with a huge red bow on top of it on the bed. I immediately knew what it was. It was another apology gift from my husband. Those kind of gifts were getting more and more frequent. My tolerance for his mental and physical pain was increasing along with my gradually growing addiction to pain killers. This time the apology gift was for him smacking me in the mouth the night before. He smacked me because I said something about him flirting with some chick in front of me at a party that we attended. We argued about it on the way home, and then he smacked me in the mouth once we were in the garage. My crying pissed him off even more, so he slammed me into the wall and told me to shut the fuck up after we walked into the house. I locked myself in the bathroom until I stopped crying, and then I took some pain killers and passed out in bed.

I slowly sat up in the bed and picked up the box. I removed the bow and opened it. Inside was a brand-new designer bag from my favorite designer. It was the one that I told him that I wanted a while back during a moment when we were getting along. Us getting along didn't happen often any longer, and it was like walking on eggshells dealing with him. I never knew when I was going to push the wrong button and make him snap and go off.

I pulled the Chanel purse out of the box and held it up to look at it. It was as beautiful as it was the day, I saw it in the store. I couldn't smile about it because my mouth was still throbbing. As much as I wanted to be excited, I couldn't because of the reason I got the bag. It seemed that the only time he bought me gifts after the marriage was to apologize for something he did. Other than that, he never gave me anything anymore. If I asked for something, it annoyed and angered him. Because of him, I felt down, low, and worthless, all the time. I had nothing going on in my life. The blog never picked up, I had no job and no money. I was completely dependent on him for everything. Anytime I tried to get into something, he talked down on it. Nothing was going the way I had planned it when I chose to marry him, but I was determined to make my marriage work.

I was thinking about getting away for a while. I figured going home for a visit would put me in a better mood. I didn't know how I would get there, but I had to come up with a plan. I needed a break from my life. I needed to be around family and friends to get my happiness back because it was gone. I decided to find some way to ask him about sending me home for a visit. I slid out of bed and walked to the bathroom to brush my teeth and wash my face. After I was done in the bathroom, I slid on my robe and slippers. I looked at myself in the bathroom mirror and touched the purple bruise by my mouth. I knew that I was going to need to cover it up, if we went out that day. I had become a master makeup artist with covering up the bruises he left on me.

I exhaled, walked out of the bathroom, walked over to my dresser, pulled out a bottle of pills, popped one, swallowed it down with some water, and then I headed downstairs to the kitchen. Orlando was in the kitchen cooking up a breakfast for the both of us. He turned and smiled at me when he saw me.

"Hey baby." he said.

I gave a slight smile and said, "Hi babe. Good morning."

"Good morning baby. Come here." he said.

I walked over to him, he grabbed my hand, pulled me to him, and kissed me. He searched my face, and then he touched the bruise by my mouth.

"Daddy is sorry." he said.

I nodded my head and looked down at the ground.

"Look at me." he said, and then he pulled my chin up so he could look me in my eyes.

"I've been fucking up. I know I have, and I've been treating you bad. You don't deserve that. You're my wife and I love you to death. You hear me?"

I nodded my head, but I didn't speak.

"I apologize about last night baby. I was drunk and I lost myself and I did some things that I shouldn't have done. I haven't been myself in this marriage at all and I've been treating you bad. I want you to know that I recognize it and I'm going to change. I can't be hurting you. I can't lose my career over the stuff I'm doing to you. I can't lose you. I'm going to get it together. I'm going to get help and I need your support on this. I need you baby, so I'm going to work on it. I promise, ok?"

I nodded my head and said, "Ok."

"I'm serious baby. Ok?"

I said, "Ok."

"You see I'm down here trying to cook breakfast for you."

"I see."

"You know I don't cook, so you gotta know that I'm serious."

"I know."

"Ok then, so forgive me please."

"Ok, I forgive you."

"Did you get the bag?"

"Yes I did. I love it. Thank you."

"I knew you would. I remember you telling me that you wanted that bag really bad."

"I did. I can't wait to show it off."

"I can't wait for you to show it off and make all these broke bitches jealous."

I laughed, and then he said, "Have a seat baby so I can make you a plate."

I walked over to the island table and sat down. Orlando walked over with a plate of food, set it in front of me, and then he kissed me.

"I love you baby."

"I love you too."

As he was walking away to make his plate, he said, "This was a lot of work. Next time I'm hiring a chef."

I chuckled as I took a bite of the burnt eggs, the overly crispy bacon, and burnt toast. I washed the nasty food down with some juice. I wished he had hired a chef so I wouldn't have had to endure eating horrible food.

"How is it babe? It's nasty?" he asked when he sat down next to me.

"No, it's delicious babe. I love it." I lied. I really wanted to throw it away or feed it to some pigs.

"Alright cool." he said.

"Babe I was wondering. Do you think we can afford to send me home?" I asked.

"For what?"

"To visit? I miss home. I miss my family."

"Yea I feel you. I miss my family too. You know what? We can both take a trip out there. I need to see my family too. We haven't seen our families since our wedding. Plus, I got some business to discuss with a few of my friends out there. I'll set it up and make it happen."

I perked up, and asked, "Really? When?"

"Soon."

"Thank you, baby!" I said excitedly. I couldn't wait to get home. I needed a break and to be around something familiar.

After we finished eating, he cleared our plates, and told me to go and get dressed while he cleaned the kitchen. I searched through my walk-in closet for a pretty sundress and a pair of heels that matched my new handbag. I got dressed, covered my bruise with some make-up and met Orlando back downstairs so we could leave.

It was warm spring day and we had the best day that we'd had together in a long time. There was no arguing and no negativity. Orlando was being his old self again. He took me to a spa to get massages, and then he took me shopping. After shopping, we went out to get lunch at one of my favorite restaurants, and then he took me to a party that one of his ball player friends was having. Lisa and the girls were there. We drank, socialized, and had a good time. There was no arguing between us at all. When we got home that night, he made love to me like he did the day we came home from our honeymoon. All was good, I was loving it, and back in love with him.

Chapter 8

Kyra

Kyra picked up the flat iron and straightened a piece of her clients hair with it. She put the hair in place, and then started on another piece. Her client was talking her ear off about her kids and husband, but Kyra's couldn't get her mind off Corey. She had been unable to get in contact with him all day, and that usually meant he was up to no good, and on some drug binge. She sent him a text message telling him to call her right away. Hours had gone by and she still hadn't heard from him. She straightened another piece of hair, pulled her phone out of her apron pocket to look at it again. Corey text back and told her that he would call her in five minutes. She put her phone back into her pocket and turned her attention back to her client.

"Are you ok girl?" her client asked.

"Yes I am." Kyra smiled.

"Oh ok. You just seem distant today."

"Oh, I'm sorry. I was in my thoughts about something, but I'm ok."

"Is everything alright?"

"Yea, everything is fine, girl."

"Okaay." her client sang.

"So what did you say that your husband did?" Kyra asked her client to deflect her attention from her.

"Girl I told him to ice my cake because I was in the shower trying to get dressed. This fool literally pulled ice cubes out of the freezer and put them on top of my freshly baked cake."

Kyra busted into laughter, "Girl no."

"Yes completely ruined my cake. I don't know what the hell he was thinking. He said he thought that is what I meant. I said nah fool put icing on the cake, as in frosting. What the hell."

"Oh my gosh. That is too funny." Kyra said through laughs.

"The ice melted all on top of the cake. Had my cake all soggy. I had to throw the whole damn cake out."

"I can't believe he did that. You should have recorded it and put it on Instagram."

"I know. I probably would have gone viral. I wanted to choke him. I was so mad, but I laughed about it later. I swear he is like having another kid in the house."

"I see." Kyra said.

"Yea, I love him, but I told him that he smokes too much weed."

Kyra laughed and turned her client around in the chair so she could look at her hair. Her client used the handheld mirror to see the back.

"Oh yes girl, this is hot. You get me right every time. Thank you."

"You're welcome." Kyra said.

She helped her client out of the chair and walked her to the front to pay. After the client paid and said her goodbye's, Kyra made her way to the back of the salon so she could return the call from Corey.

"Hey baby. I'm sorry I missed your call. I was in the middle of a meeting." he said when he answered.

"I was wondering where you were."

"Yea. A club wants to book me for a gig here. They think it's going to be big, so it will be some good money hopefully, but you know how these local club gigs go."

"I know."

He sniffled, and then he asked, "How are you? How is work going?"

"It's going good. I just finished up with one of my favorite clients."

"Which one? The old lady, the stripper, or the talkative one?" he asked.

"The talkative one. She was talking about her husband and kids. You know she always has a funny story about her husband."

"Yea, I know. You'll have to tell me about it when you get home."

"You know I will."

"I know."

"Where are you headed?"

"To my boy T's house."

"T?" Kyra asked.

She felt her house start to race. T meant trouble. Every time Corey started hanging around T, his drug addiction and drinking worsened. The two of them partied together and did drugs together and nothing good came from Corey being around him.

Corey quickly said, "Babe don't start."

"You know that I don't like you around him." Kyra said. "Corey, you know every time you start hanging with T, you get yourself into trouble."

"No I don't." Corey refuted.

"Yes you do. You know he isn't any good for no one. Is that the reason why you weren't calling me or answering my calls? Because you were off somewhere getting high with him? Or at a coke party?"

"Kyra, Stop."

"I'm serious."

"No. I got this baby. Don't trip."

"Okaay." Kyra sang.

"Alright. I just pulled up. I'll call you later."

"Ok. Oh I wanted to ask you something. There was some money missing from my stash. Have you been in it?"

"Oh yea babe. I meant to tell you. I'm sorry. My check hasn't cleared from the tour yet, so I used some to get a few things. I'll put it back though. You know that I'm good for it."

"Yea babe, just let me know next time, dang."

He sniffled, and then he said, "I got you. I love you."

"I love you too."

Chapter 9

Kyra

Kyra asked Bianca if she wanted to get some food after work. She was hungry, but also just wanted to have some girl chat. Kyra's best friend lived in Atlanta, but she had known Bianca for years through the hair industry. They too had a close friendship. She'd confided in Bianca over a few things, but she never talked to her about Corey's drug addiction. Kyra's best friend in Atlanta was the only one who knew about that. Bianca had become someone that Kyra could chat with about normal day to day stuff and get a couple of laughs.

Bianca agreed to go out to eat, so they decided to go to a seafood restaurant Uptown and sit in a booth on the rooftop. Kyra ordered a salad, and Bianca ordered fish and shrimp.

"You really love seafood, don't you girl?" Kyra asked.

"I really do. It's my favorite food besides soul food."

"We should take a trip down to Chicago sometime, so I can bring you to Pappadeaux's"

"What's that?"

"It's this really good seafood restaurant."

"Girl, how do you know? You don't even eat meat?"

Kyra laughed and said, "Corey took me there once. I didn't eat any meat dishes, but he did, and he has been talking about it ever since."

Bianca laughed and said, "Oh ok. How is he doing anyway?"

"He's been good."

"He's home, right?"

"Yea. He has been back for a few weeks now."

"I know you're happy. I know how much you be missing him."

"Girl, I really do. It gets lonely when he's gone. Especially when he is gone for months on tour with someone."

"I thought he was a DJ for one person."

"He is mainly, but he picked up a few other artists that he travels with."

"Oh ok. He's getting that money."

"Yea he is, but even that be iffy sometimes. It depends. Right now he is doing really good though."

"That's good."

"So what's going on with your boo?" Kyra asked.

"Girl Andre gets on my last nerve."

Kyra laughed and took a sip water. "What did he do now?"

"What doesn't he do, girl?" Bianca chuckled. "If it wasn't for that good ass dick, I would have been gone."

Kyra laughed and said, "You always say that."

"I'm serious. You remember I told you about that chick I got into it with on Facebook over him."

"Yup, I remember."

"After that, some other chick got to talking shit on my Instagram account."

"Oh my goodness." Kyra said.

"He sells them weed. I know they're his clients and fucks them from time to time, but he's supposed to keep them in check. I keep telling them bitches that's my dick and I ain't going nowhere."

Kyra chuckled and said, "I don't understand y'all situation. Are y'all together or not?"

"Girl, we're together when we're together, but he does him and I do me. We just make sure that we respect each other and always put each other first over anything."

"So you're basically in an open relationship?" Kyra asked, and then she took a bite of food.

Bianca took a sip of her drink, and then she said, "Basically, but he is supposed to keep them bitches in check. His hoes are never supposed to come for me, and who I deal with is never supposed to come for him. He just can't keep his hoes in line." She took a few bites of food and dabbed her mouth with a napkin.

Kyra chuckled, took a sip of her drink, and then she said, "Y'all situation is a little messy sis."

"It wouldn't be if his bitches would know their place and stay in it."

Kyra laughed, and then Bianca aid, "For real girl. The problem is these chicks be thinking they have more with him than what it is. They're not realizing that they're just temporary. I'm the permanent fixture in his life. They are just some little toys that he plays with every now and then."

"So are y'all always going to be in an open relationship?"

"I don't know. I mean, I thought about asking him to make it official, but I know that he doesn't want that. We've already been down that road, and I would rather him fuck with other women in the open, than cheat on me and do it beyond my back. Plus it gives me the freedom to do what I want to do and play when I want to too, so it's kind of the perfect situation."

"Do you ever worry about him brining something home?"

"Nah, he knows better. We both stay strapped up. Hell, we go and buy condoms together."

Kyra said, "Y'all crazy."

"But we love each other, and it works."

"I hear you. Hey, if you like it, I love it."

"The other women is not my main concern with him anyway. My issue with him is this hustling thing. He is the most broke drug dealer in the world. Because he is always wasting his money on bullshit. He always needs some money for something. I done spent so much money on this dude. I just need for him to get a real job."

"You're giving him money sis?"

"Yes girl all the fucking time. I just gave him two hundred dollars today. He said he needed it for his son. Not to mention all the times I've given him money because he fucked up all his. I pay his phone bill, I buy his clothes, and he basically lives with me. Most of his shit is at my house."

"Sis, that is your son." Kyra said.

Bianca said, "Girl no that's my Zaddy. I love him."

"You're taking care of a grown ass man."

"I'm just helping him out when he needs me."

"I hear you." Kyra said, and then she put her napkin in her plate.

"Damn you're full already?"

"I am girl."

"You barely ate anything."

"I know, but I can't take another bite."

"That's because you're so little. You eat like a bird. You skinny bitches don't know how to get it in with some good food."

Kyra laughed and said. "Whatever."

"Anyways, Zaddy is coming over to my house tonight. I'm going to cook for him, and then he is going to give me some of that good good."

"I bet he is." Kyra said.

"Yea girl, so let's get out of here. I've got to run by the grocery store."

"Yea I got to get home and get dinner ready for Corey."

"Have you seen Adara's baby yet?"

"Not yet. He is still in the NICU, so I've been waiting for her to bring him home. Have you been up to the hospital?"

"I've been waiting for her to bring him home too. I talked to her though. I saw Wesley too and he said the baby was healthy and doing good, so I can't wait to see him."

"Yea I can't wait either. Where did you see Wesley?"

"He was with my brother."

"Oh ok. Well, thanks for having dinner with me sis. I needed some girl chat."

"Girl, thank you. I needed some girl chat too."

The ladies asked for take-out boxes, packed up their food, paid the waitress, and left the restaurant. The dinner with Bianca helped keep Kyra's mind off Corey and worrying about where he was. She headed home and hoped to see Corey there. That would put her heart and mind at ease.

Chapter 10

Adara

I was stressed out to say the least. I was home, but my new baby boy was still in the NICU at the hospital. I was worried about him because he wasn't doing well. He was breathing on his own, but he had dropped weight from four pounds back down to three pounds. The doctor told me that he was not doing well with eating, so he wasn't gaining weight as he was supposed to. I was home taking care of Ava, running back and forth to the hospital to check on my baby, and dealing with the salon. Wes was no help at all. He was in and out of the house running the streets, and he only visited our baby boy once since I'd given birth to him.

Most days I wanted to punch Wes in the face. Especially the day his other baby's mother Leslie gave birth to her baby.

Our baby had finally been released from the hospital, and Wes was gone the entire night. Our son was up crying most of the day and night. I fed him, I held him, I changed him, I bathed him, I walked with him, I even sung to him, and he would not stop crying. I text Wes and asked him to come home to help me. He told me that he was coming. Two hours later, no Wes, and I was still dealing with our crying baby.

I called Wes. No answer, but the he called back an hour later. I told him that I needed him to come home. He said that he was coming in an hour. Two hours later, no Wes. I called again. This time I was pissed. I fussed at him about him not being there and leaving me there alone with our daughter and a crying baby. He told me to calm down, and he would be there. By two o'clock in the morning, I had finally got our son to settle down for an hour. He was back up at three o'clock, and then I got him back to sleep by four. Wes walked in an hour after that. I was livid. He had the nerve to walk in the door at five o'clock in the morning.

I heard him creep into the house. I sat up in my bed and clicked on the lamp. I rested my back on the headboard and folded my arm across my breasts. I was stressed, tired, angry, and ready for war. Wes walked into the room, looked at me, and then dropped his head. I know that he could tell by the look on my face that it was not going to be a peaceful night.

He said, "Babe I'm sorry."

"Where have you been Wes? Huh? Where the fuck have you been? Five o'clock? Really?"

"I know. I'm sorry."

"I've been up all night dealing with your son, and you come walking up in here at five o'clock in the morning like I haven't been calling and texting you all night?"

"I'm sorry-"

"Whoever the fuck she is, go back to her. Is it Leslie? Huh?"

"No. I was getting money."

"Until five o'clock in the morning Wesley?"

"Yea. Money doesn't stop."

"You're a fucking liar."

"I gotta get this money. I can't drop what I'm doing to come home because the baby is crying."

"How about get a real fucking job Wes. How about be at home with your woman and your kids. Especially your son who needs special attention. The son *you wanted*. The relationship *you wanted*. Remember that?"

"You're going to keep throwing that shit in my face?"

"Yes I am. Because for some reason, I think you forgot."

"I didn't forget shit, but I got to take care of my business, so that you eat, and they eat."

"You're supposed to be a father to them and a man to me. That is the problem here. You're not doing that."

"Uuugh Adara. You want me to do so fucking much."

"What is so fucking much? Asking you to be home at a decent time at night? Asking you to help me with your fucking kids? Asking you to get a decent fucking job so you're not running around in these streets or coming home at all hours of the night. That is asking for too much?"

"All I'm saying is I'm trying to do me."

"*YOU* said that you wanted me back. *YOU* told me that you wanted your family back. *YOU* told me that you wanted our baby, and now you've got the nerve to stand here and tell me that your trying to do you?" I paused, and then I said, "I can't."

I could feel tears beginning to form and I needed to get up and get away from him. I snatched the blanket off my legs and stood up. I walked towards the door. Wes grabbed my arm, so I stopped walking.

Without looking at him, I said, "Don't fucking touch me Wes. Just leave me alone because I really want to punch the shit out of you right now."

"Aight." he said. He let go of my arm, and then I walked into the living room. I grabbed a blanket out of the hall closet and laid down on the couch. I heard Wes go into the bathroom. I listened to him take a shower, and then come out to the living room.

He whispered, "Adara."

I stayed silent, and then he said, "Baby I'm sorry."

He kissed me on the forehead, stood up, and went into the room. After I heard him get into my bed, I allowed myself to fall asleep.

***

About an hour and a half later, I felt him shaking me to wake me up.

"Adara." he whispered.

After he whispered my name again, I groaned, "Hmmmm."

"Baby I got to go."

I turned over and asked, "Back out to the streets already? Really Wes?"

"Nah. Leslie is at the hospital having the baby. I'm about to head up there."

"Well, at least she got you to go to the hospital on time for the birth of her baby."

"Adara stop."

"Whatever. Congratulations."

"I love you baby, ok? I'll be home tonight. I promise."

"Yea whatever."

"Kiss the babies for me. I'll see you tonight."

I listened to Wes walk out of the door, and then I stood up, folded the blanket, walked into the bedroom, and laid down in my bed. I was still very angry, but I knew I needed the rest so I could get prepared for my day with my crying newborn and my daughter.

Before I could get back into a good sleep, my son started crying again. I scratched my head, and then I slowly crawled out of bed to go and get him from his crib. I didn't know what I had got myself into having another baby by Wes. I should've known that I was going to be doing it alone, but no, I wanted to try and be a family. I was feeling serious regrets at that moment. I just sat on the couch, held my baby, and cried with him.

Chapter 11

Adara

Wes and I got into a huge fight the next day. I was at home with our crying child all night again, and he was at the hospital with his other baby's mom. As a woman, I understood that she was having a baby, but I needed him at home with me and his crying baby. I was irritated at the fact that he was having a baby with her anyway, so to add fuel to the fire, he had the nerve to show up the next day. Not even in the morning. It was almost afternoon when he made it back home. Maybe I was being a little petty. I was in my feelings about him spending all that time at the hospital with his side chick but had the nerve to not even be there for me when our son was being born.

When he walked into my house, I said nothing to him. I had just got our son to go to sleep and I was making Ava something to eat for lunch. She was watching a children's television show in the living room and playing with her toys. I was in the kitchen making peanut butter and jelly sandwich with sliced apples. My cousin Nikita was going to be stopping by later that day to visit and help me with the baby, so I was also preparing something for us to snack while we chatted. Ava dropped her toys, jumped up, and ran to him when he walked in the door.

"Daddy!" she said.

"Hey baby girl." he said, and then he scooped her up in his arms and kissed her on the cheek. After hugging her, he put her back down to her feet and told her to go and play. He made his way into the kitchen to talk to me.

"Hey baby." he said. He wrapped his arms around me to hug me, but I shrugged his arms off me and walked to the refrigerator. I pulled a few things out and walked back over to the counter.

"You're not speaking to me?" he asked as he followed me back over to the counter. I remained silent until he said my name.

"Adara."

I looked at him and said, "I don't have nothing to say to you."

"Really Adara? You're going to act like this because I was at the hospital watching my baby being born."

"You weren't even there for your son to be born and haven't been here since he was born."

"You starting that shit? I'm not about to do this with you."

I yelled, "Do what!? Talk about you neglecting me and your children!"

"I'm not doing this! I'm out!"

"Leave then! That's what you've been doing!"

Wes stormed out of the house and slammed the door behind him. My son started crying right after the door slammed. I slammed my knife down on the kitchen counter and yelled, "Uuuuugh!"

I covered my face with my hands and let some tears fall while listening to my son cry in the other room. Ava walked into the kitchen and said, "Mama baby is crying."

I said, "I know baby. I'm coming to get him."

I wiped the tear with my hands and made my way to the bedroom to get my son. I picked him up, laid him across my chest and began bouncing him while walking with him. He started to calm down once he was in my arms. I was so frustrated with Wes that I wanted to scream, but I had to hold it together for my kids. Once I got him to calm down, I put him in his bouncy seat and turned on the vibration. I set him in the kitchen with me, so I could finish preparing lunch for Ava and for Nikita's visit.

My phone started ringing and I was shocked to see who was calling. I picked up the phone and said, "Sis! I'm surprised to hear from you."

I couldn't believe that she was calling. I hadn't really talked to her since we'd had a slight argument over her husband's cheating allegation that went viral.

Chanel laughed and said, "I know. I'm sorry. I know I was short with you the last time we talked."

"It's ok sis. I understand."

"I miss you."

"I miss you too! When are you coming home to see me, your niece, and your new nephew?"

"That is why I'm calling. I'm coming sooner than you think."

"What! When?"

"This weekend."

"Oh my God really sis?"

"Yes!"

"I can't wait!"

"I can't wait either. I miss you; I miss home, I miss everybody."

"We miss you too."

"I'll call you when I touch down."

"Ok see you soon sis. I love you."

"I love you too."

I continued smile as I placed my phone back on the counter. That news put me back into good spirits.

"Your aunt will be here soon," I said to my son, and then I got a text from Nikita telling me that she was pulling up. I picked up the car seat and walked with my son to the door. I watched Nikita park in my driveway, get out of her car, and walk towards me.

"Hey cousin." she said when she reached me. She hugged me, and then she took the baby from my hands. She followed me in while holding the car seat.

"Look at him looking so handsome. He's gained a lot of weight girl."

"I know. I'm so happy."

"I am too. I was worried about my little cousin."

"He's ok besides all the crying. He is eating a lot more and has gained weight. The doctors says he is doing really good. He just cries so much. I'm surprised that he isn't crying now."

"I hope my baby doesn't cry a lot."

"I'm praying that he doesn't."

"Nikita sat down and put the bouncy seat in front of her. She gently put my baby boy into the vibrating seat, and then she sat back in the chair. She was almost full term pregnant and her belly was huge. She looked like she was ready to pop.

"You're due soon right?"

"Yes. I'm almost done, and then I can have my body back."

I laughed and said, "I know what you mean."

She asked, "Where's Wes?"

"Girl I don't know. Somewhere in the streets like he's been."

"Wow really? Still?"

"Yup. He was just here not too long ago, but he got mad and left."

"What the hell does was he mad about?"

"My question exactly. I was upset because he was out all night again last night, and then he got mad at me."

"How is he going to be mad because your mad?"

I said, "Right, so he stormed out of here leaving me with these kids again."

Nikita said, "That is not right cousin."

"I know. His other baby mom had her baby."

"Leslie?"

"Yup."

"Oh wow. How do you feel about it?"

"Honestly, I don't have good feelings about it. I'm just so sick of him right now. Honestly, I'm starting to regret that I ever made the decision to have this baby."

"Don't feel like that because his dumb ass is acting up. This baby is a blessing."

"It sure doesn't feel like that right now. If I would've gone through with my plan to have an abortion, I wouldn't be dealing with this right now."

"Yea girl, but you have a beautiful baby. Yea your baby daddy is a bum ass dude, but that is beside the point. You were blessed with a handsome son."

"Listen to you. That pregnancy got you all spiritual and emotional."

Nikita laughed, "Shut up cousin. I'm serious. My son is by a bum ass dude, but I love my son. What his daddy does has nothing to do with my baby."

"True."

"I'm glad this baby ain't by Jakari even though he thinks it is."

I laughed, and then I said, "I hear you girl."

"On another note, Fuck Wes. How dare his bum ass leave you here with these two kids. We should call our cousin Joe to beat his ass." she said.

I laughed again, and said, "I can always count on you to make me laugh and make me feel better girl. Thank you."

"You're welcome cousin. You know I got you."

"Anyways. Guess who I talked to today?"

"Who?"

"Chanel."

"Ah damn. Long time no hear. How has she been?"

"I don't know girl. The last time I talked to her was after you told me about her husband's cheating scandal. We got into it, and then we didn't talk for a while. She called me out of the blue today saying that she is going to be here this weekend."

"What!?" Nikita asked.

"Yup. I'm excited. I haven't seen her since the wedding, and I miss her."

"Oooo girl I can't wait to see her cause I got some questions."

"Girl don't do that."

"Don't do what? Shit inquiring minds wants to know and I'm asking for a friend."

I chuckled and said, "Stop Nikita."

"Whaaaaatttt?" Nikita sang.

"We're not going to ask her about any of that stuff that happened with her husband. We're not going to bring that up at all. We're just going to enjoy having her home, having some girls time, and some girl chat."

"What is girl chat without addressing the gossip?"

"Nikita."

"Whaaat?"

"No. You two have been in a good place since the wedding, so let's just keep it that way. Take your petty hat off, and put your petty juice down, and be nice."

"Can I at least keep on my petty shoes?"

I laughed and said, "Nikita!"

She laughed and saaang, "Okaaaaayy."

"Thank you."

"It's going to be hard, but I'll be good. Only because I love you."

"Yea ok. You wouldn't want anyone to do that to you and I wouldn't let anyone do that to you."

"Alright. I'll leave it alone."

"Good. Thank you. Now, are you hungry? I made lunch."

"Girl you know me, and this baby are always hungry."

"Ok good because I made your favorite. Do you mind feeding the baby while I get the food ready?"

"Not at all. I got to get practice again anyways."

I stood up, gave her a bottle to give him, and finished preparing lunch.

Chapter 12

Chanel

I stared out of the window of the large airplane as it descended from the sky and made its way to the ground. The aircraft was landing at the airport back home. I was in my thoughts about my marriage to Orlando and all the things I had been going through with him. Flash backs of the last fight we had flooded my mind. He had promised me that he wouldn't touch me again, but he did. The memory of him smacking me down to the ground, and then standing over me yelling at me while I held my face and cried kept popping into my head. I never expected him to become the monster that he'd become. I never expected him to be the cheater he'd become either.

On top of the abuse, there were multiple allegations of him cheating from different sources. Online blog sites, haters, and fans. Not to mention, the few women who had been bold or rude enough to approach me by sending DM's on social media. I questioned myself why I kept accepting his apologies, forgiving him, and then allowing him to do it again. I questioned myself why I kept choosing to stay.

I closed my eyes to push the thoughts out of my head, and then I felt Orlando move. He was asleep in the seat next to me on the plane. He had his head rested on my shoulder and his fingers were intertwined with mine. His hand was on the bottom and mine was on the top. The bling from my huge wedding ring caught my attention. I looked down at our hands intertwined, and then I focused my attention on my ring. I remembered how I felt like I was the luckiest girl in the world to be marry Orlando King; one of the richest players in the league. I remembered how proud I felt to show off my huge ring to the other wives and girlfriends in the league. Especially the groupies and wanna be's that would be in the parties, clubs, and on social media. I questioned was it all worth it. Was the money and rich life worth all the pain and suffering?

Orlando moved again, sat up in his seat, and then he rubbed his eyes. He yawned and said, "Damn we here?"

"Yes." I said.

"Damn I was sleepy as hell." he said.

I wanted to say something about the reason why he was so sleepy, but I decided not to. I didn't want to set him off and start an argument. He seemed to be in a good mood, and I wanted to keep it that way. I was back home and ready to have a good time with my friends and family. I didn't want to be fighting with Orlando about something he did. Although I was extremely irritated about being out until the wee hours of the morning the night before again, I decided to keep it to myself. I was learning to pick my battles when dealing with Orlando. No need to show up with a black eye on an account of confronting Orlando about his bullshit.

I twiddled my wedding ring with my thumb, and then I began gathering my things. I listened to the pilot over the loudspeaker and Orlando talking about something I didn't really care about as the plane came to a stop.

I felt Orlando kiss my cheek, and then he asked, "Are you ok?"

"Yes."

"Are you sure?" he asked.

"Yes." I mustered up a fake smile.

"Ok good. Are you happy to be home baby?"

"Extremely."

"Good. I'm happy to be home too."

We gathered our things and exited the plane. I was still in my thoughts as we made our way through the airport to the baggage claim area. I couldn't wait to get to the hotel room so I could pop another pain pill. I'd been fiending for one the entire plane ride. After we retrieved our luggage, we headed out of the airport to the rental car place to pick up our vehicle. I called Adara shortly after we got into the vehicle.

"Hello?" Adara answered.

"Guess what chick?" I asked.

"What?"

"I'm here!" I said excitedly.

"For real!?" Adara asked.

"Yup! We're on the way to the hotel now."

"Oh my God! Yaaay!"

"I know. I'm too excited."

"Me too! Perfect timing too. My mom is taking the kids tonight, so I can get a break and have some me time. So, we can go out and do something tonight."

"Ok cool. Well, I'm going to the hotel to get dressed, and then I'll be over."

"I can't wait to see you! Nikita will be here too."

"I can't wait to see you. Nikita too."

"I know you miss home if you're excited to see Nikita." Adara said.

I laughed and said, "I know right. I'll see you soon."

"Ok."

I hung up my phone call and heard Orlando on the phone with one of his friends, so I decided to call my mom and let her know that I had made it safe. When my mom answered, I chatted about the plane ride, and then I told her that I was going to hang out with Adara. I promised that we would be over the next day to visit since it was later in the evening. My mom told me that she loved me and to be safe. We disconnected the call just as Orlando was finishing up his conversation with his friend. I heard him say that he would see them in a minute and to be ready.

He disconnected and said, "That was Deon babe. He is, too pumped that I'm here."

"Oh yea?"

"Yea. He said to tell you that he said hi. He wants us to stop by tomorrow his wife and kids can see us."

"Ok."

I felt an unnerving feeling in my stomach. I knew him and Deon together meant trouble. Nothing good was going to come from that union. Whenever they got together, it was nothing but trouble. Orlando was liable to wake up the next day not knowing where he was, who he was with, or how he got there. Then, they both would have to make up excuses to tell their wives.

"How are the newlyweds doing anyway?" I asked.

"Deon says they are doing really good. I can't believe my boy got married and didn't tell anybody."

"They eloped in Vegas, right?"

"Yup. I can't believe he did it."

"Well, it was time. He has two kids with her. I don't see why it took him so long to begin with."

"Aye, my boy has always been a playboy. I didn't think he would ever settle down. I probably inspired him."

"Right, so you're hanging out with him tonight."

"Yes. I can't wait. I haven't seen him in a minute."

"I bet."

"What is that supposed to mean."

"Nothing."

"Nah, what was that supposed to mean?"

"Nothing."

"Aight. Were you talking to Adara?"

"Yup."

"What's up with her?"

"She is excited that I'm here and can't wait to see me."

"Yea. I know she's happy that you're here. It's been a while since she's seen you."

"Since the wedding."

"I know."

"I told my mom that we would be by tomorrow."

"Ok."

"So, what're you and Deon getting into tonight?"

"I don't know yet. Why?"

"Hmm."

"What?"

"Nothing." I said. I pulled out my phone and began scrolling through my social media timeline. I decided not to get into it. The last thing I wanted to do was start an argument with him. I had already said too much.

We arrived at the hotel a short time later. Orlando sat down on the couch and turned on the television. He had his focus on his phone and the person that he was sending text messages to. I went into the bathroom to take a shower and get dressed. Orlando's attention was on his phone the entire time until I walked past him. I was walking to my luggage to pull out a pair of shoes to wear. He smelled the scent of my perfume and looked up. He watched me searching through my luggage.

"You're wearing that?" he asked.

"Yea." I said as I pulled the shoes I wanted to wear out of the bag.

"Why are you wearing that top?" he asked.

I looked down at the black top I was wearing. I was a backless blouse with a plunging neckline. I admit it was a bit sexy, but I was going to hang with the girls, so I wanted to look somewhat sexy. They hadn't seen me in a long time. I was wearing a pair of skinny leg jeans and a blouse. I felt like it was appropriate attire for what I was going to do.

I looked at my image in the mirror on the wall and asked, "What's wrong with it?"

"It's too sexy for you to be wearing just to go and visit with your friends."

I giggled and said, "No it's not. It's simple blouse and a pair of jeans."

"I don't like the shirt."

"Why?"

"You got your back all out and your cleavage showing."

I giggled again and said, "It's a blouse Orlando."

"It's showing too much. If you lean forward your nipple might pop out, and then you got your back all out for all the thirsty ass dudes out there to look at. Take that shit off."

"Seriously? I've worn tops and dresses more revealing than this going out with you."

"Right, when you're with me. You're not wearing no slutty shit to go hang out with your friends. Take that shit off." he said angrily.

"Whatever Orlando." I said with a roll of my eyes. I put my shoes on and started walking towards the counter where my purse was. He jumped up and grabbed me by my arm.

"I said take this off."

"For what? I'm already dressed. I don't want to be late. Please let me go."

"Stop playing with me and take this shit off." he said.

I sighed and calmly said, "You're tripping for nothing."

Orlando smacked me and threw me down on the floor. He grabbed me by the top and dragged me back through the room. He picked me up, and then slammed me on the bed. He used all his strength to rip the top off me, and then he balled it up and threw it at my face.

"Now change into something else like I said!" he growled at me.

A silent tear ran down my cheek as I slowly got up off the bed, walked to my luggage to find a new top to wear. He had just ruined my three-hundred-dollar top and smacked me so hard I had a slight headache.

He kept his eyes on me the entire time I searched for a new shirt to wear. I found a less revealing form fitted top and put it on, and then I went back into the bathroom to fix my makeup. It had tear streaks in it, and I couldn't go outside like that. He watched from the other room as I reapplied my make-up. He stayed silent the entire time and there was so much tension and negative energy coming from where he was sitting. I just hoped he didn't try to pick another fight and I could get out of there. I did everything in a hurry, grabbed my purse, and headed to the door.

"Be back here at a decent time." he said.

I didn't respond. I just walked out of the room.

Chapter 13

Adara

DING DONG

I heard the doorbell and did a light jog to the door. I looked through the peep hole to make sure that it was her. A huge smile spread across my face when I saw her standing on the other side of the door.

I swung the door open and yelled, "Sister!"

"Sister!" she responded.

We threw our arms open and we squeezed each other in a tight hug. When we released each other, I said,

"Look at you. You've gotten so thin." "What have you been doing?" I asked as I shut the door.

"Well, you know. Nothing much really. Just being a wife. Trying to keep my husband happy and my house clean."

"I hear that girl. Well, you're looking good." I said.

I didn't mean it though. Chanel's size was alarming to me. She was thinner than she'd ever been. I knew that was a sign that something wasn't right, but Chanel was trying to hide behind a smile. According to the media and the blogs Orlando was still up to no good. I decided not to address any of it to avoid what happened the last time I'd brought up Orlando's mess.

"You're looking good too sis. Especially after having your second baby." she said.

"Well, thank you. Trust me, I'm no stranger to a good workout out. I get it in when I can. With and without the babies. Anything that I can do. I go on walks with them, I work out while their napping, I work out when their up and occupied, sometimes I incorporate them. Shoot mama gotta keep this figure right."

"That is really good. I admire that." she said.

"Thank you."

"You're welcome."

"Well come inside." I said.

Chanel followed me through the house and looked around. "It has been a long time since I've been over here. You've changed some things around. It looks really nice in here."

"Well, my house is not even close to being as big and fabulous as your house, but I did buy all new furniture and appliances, I painted, and then I changed things around for the kids."

"It's not as big as the house that I'm living in, but it's yours, and it's beautiful."

I made a facial expression that said that I was taken aback by what Chanel said, and then I said, "Wow, I can't believe *you* just said that."

Chanel laughed and said, "What? Don't be so shocked."

"How can I not be shocked? Mrs. Materialistic. All things must be expensive and luxurious honey."

"Yea. Well…" Chanel said, and then she shrugged her shoulders.

"Well, have a seat. Would you like a drink?"

"Yes."

"Will wine do?"

"Of course."

"Ok."

It's not expensive wine."

"I don't care."

"*Really?* Who is this person? Where is Chanel?"

She chuckled and said, "Shut up. I'm right here."

"Uh uh. I don't know you."

"Whatever." she said.

The doorbell rang again, and then I said, "Oh that's Nikita. Let me get the door.

Chanel stood up to greet Nikita when she walked in.

"Hey cousin!" I said when I opened the door.

"Hey!" Nikita said, and then she turned her attention to Chanel. "Hey girl! Welcome back!" Nikita said as she walked in.

"Hey girl! Oh my God! Look at your belly!" Chanel said before hugging her.

"I know girl. I'm about to pop."

"When are you due?"

"Soon. I can't wait."

"So you're having another one by Jakari, huh?"

"Girl it's a long story. We'll get into that later, but it's good to see you. You've gotten so little."

"I know. That's what everyone keeps telling me." Chanel said, and then she turned to me and said, "Why didn't you tell me that she was pregnant Adara?"

"I didn't get the chance to."

"Wow. Congratulations." she said to Nikita.

"Thank you." Nikita replied.

"You're welcome."

I said, "I made reservations at your favorite restaurant Chanel."

"Oh my gosh! Really?"

"Um hum!"

"I haven't been there in a long time! Thank you." Chanel said, and then she hugged me.

"You know I got you sister. You know that you couldn't leave here without eating your favorite dish. "Well, ladies have a seat. We have a few minutes before we need to leave." I said.

I closed and locked my door, and then I made my way to the kitchen. Chanel and Nikita walked into the living room, sat down, and began to chat. When I returned, I handed a glass of wine to Chanel, and then I sat down with a glass of wine for myself in hand.

"I'm jealous." Nikita said.

"You don't have too much longer." I said.

"Are you going to breast feed?" Chanel asked.

"No. I don't like it. I tried with my son and it hurt."

"Girl, how long ago was that?" I asked.

"Eight years ago, but that's beside the point."

We began laughing, and then I said, "You've got to at least try."

"Nope. I'm not." Nikita chuckled, and then she turned to Chanel and asked, "When are you about to have some babies?"

"I don't know yet. I'm still getting settled into married life and being an athletes wife. Plus, I don't think that we're ready for kids right now."

"I understand. Don't rush. Trust me. I wish I still had a free life without children sometimes." Nikita said.

"I do too." I said.

Orlando got all those kids anyway." Nikita said.

I could tell that Chanel felt slightly irritated by Nikita's comment about the number of kids Orlando had, but she ignored it and said, "That he does."

"How many does he have? Like six and a possible?" Nikita asked. Leave it up to her to ask something or say something inappropriate.

"Nikita." I said.

"Oops. I'm sorry girl. No disrespect." Nikita said.

"It's ok. That is about right. I don't know about the possible, but he does have six children."

"Oh I thought that I heard he had a baby on the way or something like that."

"I don't know anything about that."

"Nikita." I said.

"Oh. I'm sorry. My bad girl." Nikita said.

"It's ok."

"Well, how is married life? Is it hard being a stepmom to all his kids?"

I knew Chanel's irritation was growing because mine was. Nikita was straight killing the vibe single handedly. Chanel ignored it and answered the question.

"Married life has its ups and downs, but for the most part it's good. The kids aren't around a lot, but when they are, it can be a little crazy. Nothing that I can't handle though."

"Oh ok. I wouldn't know what to do with all those kids girl. He got a whole damn tribe." Nikita laughed.

Chanel chuckled, and then she asked, "Is that going to be your last baby?"

"Yes. I ain't having no more after this one."

"I'm surprised Jakari doesn't have a whole damn tribe." Chanel said.

"What is that supposed to mean?" Nikita asked.

Chanel hit way below the belt with that one, but Nikita deserved it. I almost laughed, but I caught myself. I knew the conversation was about to get out of hand, so I intervened. I didn't want the good vibes from the wedding to wear off of them and they go back to their normal bickering. I wanted to keep the peace. It felt good to have them getting along for once.

"Ok, ladies. Let's get out of here and head to the restaurant." I said. I stood up, and then they did the same and followed me to the door.

Chapter 14

Chanel

I looked down at my phone again. There was another text message from Orlando asking me where I was. I had already told him that I was at a restaurant with Adara, but he wanted to know where. I didn't want to tell him where I was because I didn't want him to pop up acting crazy. He had already pulled a stunt like that when I was out with Lisa and the wives back in New York. I didn't want him embarrassing me in front of Adara and Nikita. Plus, I knew that I wouldn't hear the end of it. If Adara knew the truth about what was really going on in our marriage, she would give me a mouth full and I didn't want to hear it. She already didn't approve of my marriage to Orlando.

I replied to Orlando's text message telling him that I didn't know where I was, and then I put my phone on the table. I turned my attention back to Adara and Nikita. They were talking about some salon gossip.

Adara turned to me and said, "Oh I forgot to tell you that I invited my friend Kyra. I hope you don't mind."

"Oh that's fine. Who is she?"

"She works at my salon. She is a friend of Bianca's. Really cool girl. I'm sure you will like her."

"Ok. Well, if you like her, I'm sure I will."

"Is everything ok with you sis? You seem a little distant."

"Oh yea. I'm fine." I said, and then I took a sip from my glass of wine. "How are you and Wes?" I asked.

Adara rolled her eyes, took a sip of her wine, and then set the wine glass back on the table. "I don't even want to think about him."

"What? I thought things were working out with you two?"

"Yea well…" Adara shrugged her shoulders, picked up her wine and took another sip. "I don't even know what to say." she said.

Nikita chimed in and said, "Girl his punk ass is back to his same old bullshit."

"Oh no sis. I was hoping that he had turned over a new leaf and you would be the next one walking down the aisle."

"Uhhhh, no wedding bells for me. Let's just say he is married to the streets."

"Wait. What do you mean streets? Is he selling drugs again?"

"I guess so. I mean I don't know what he's doing. I know that he isn't working."

"Seriously?"

"Yup."

Just then, Kyra walked inside the restaurant. Adara waved her over to the table. She smiled and walked over to where we were sitting. She was beautiful. Caramel complexion, beautiful clear skin, pretty naturally curly hair. She was a natural beauty and walked with so much grace and poise.

"Hey ladies!" she said when she walked up.

"Hey!" we responded.

Kyra hugged Adara and Nikita, and then Adara said, "Kyra this is my sister Chanel, Chanel this is my friend Kyra."

"A pleasure to meet you, and congrats on your wedding. I heard all about it." Kyra said as she shook my hand. "Hopefully good things." I responded.

Kyra laughed and said, "Amazing things. A woman can only dream to have a wedding like yours." Her voice was so soft and sweet, her vibe was so relaxed. I liked her already.

"Aww you're so sweet. Thank you." I said. She looked at Adara and said, "I like her already."

Adara said, "I told you that you would."

Kyra walked over to the empty chair next to Chanel and sat down. "Catch me up on the convo. she said.

"We were talking about Wes, but we don't need to talk about that anymore." Adara said.

I looked down at my phone and read a text message from Orlando. He was demanding to know where I was at. *Uuugh* I thought. He was getting on my nerves. Orlando was determined to ruin my fun night with my friends. He was on a mission to kill my whole vibe, and I was trying not to let him do that. He was supposed to be out enjoying himself with his friends, but instead he was worried about me and what I was doing. I was so sure once he got around Deon, he wouldn't had been thinking about me, but I guess I'd thought wrong. I turned my phone face side down on the table and rejoined the conversation with the ladies. Orlando wasn't going to spoil my time back home and my night out with my friends. He had already tried to and luckily, I'd escaped that. It could had gone way worse.

"Are you alright sis?" Adara asked me again. She noticed that my demeanor had changed.

"Yes, I'm fine." I replied.

"Are you sure?"

"Yea girl. I'm good." I said.

The other ladies listened quietly, but they didn't intervene.

Adara's phone caught her attention. She excused herself from the table to answer the call. I watched her walk away, and then I picked up my phone to see if Orlando called again. I saw two missed calls. I rolled my eyes and continued to ignore him. I put my phone back on the table and focused on enjoying my night.

Chapter 15

Adara

"Hello?" I answered and I made my way to a quiet area of the restaurant. I saw that it was my mom calling and I hoped there was nothing wrong with the kids. *Lord I hope nothing happened with the kids.* I thought.

"Hey daughter. Are you still with Chanel?"

"Yes. What's wrong? Is everything ok with the kids?

"Oh yea, everything is fine. They're with their glam-mom." I laughed at my mom calling herself glam mom. It was a new age saying that was created for grandmothers who still felt young and fabulous.

"You and this glam-mom thing." I chuckled.

"Girl I'm still young, fine, and popping. You ain't going to make me an old woman."

I chuckled and then I asked, "What's wrong?"

"I thought you said Wes was coming to get the kids around nine o'clock. It' almost ten and he still isn't here yet."

"What?" I asked. I looked at my phone and noticed the time. It was five minutes to ten. I didn't even realize that it was that late. I felt instant irritation because I asked Wes to be on time. My mom had something to do in the morning and she didn't want to be up all-night waiting for me to pick the kids up.

"I told you that I had something to do in the morning and I didn't want to be up all night." my mother said.

"I know; I know mom. Ugh. Let me call you right back mom okay?"

"Okay." my mother said.

I hung up the call and tapped Wes's name on my phone to speed dial his number. I used to have his name programmed in my phone as *Bae* before their first child, but I changed it after I got into that fight with his other baby mom Leslie. The ghetto, ratchet girl that ended our relationship.

"He's probably with her." I said to myself as I listened to his phone ring through to voicemail. I hung up on his voicemail and called again. No answer. I hung up again, rolled my eyes, and exhaled loudly. I started pacing back and forth to calm my nerves.

"He's just got to find a way to ruin my night." I said to myself. I was beyond frustrated as I sent a text message to Wes.

You were supposed to pick up the kids from my mom before 10 Wes.

"Ugh." I grunted. I knew Wes's no call no show meant that my night out with my girls was about to end. I was irritated at how selfish and immature Wes could be. I never got out of the house, and the one night I had the chance to enjoy myself, he decided to pull some dumb mess.

Chanel was watching me pace back and forth. She got up to walk over to make sure everything was alright.

"What's wrong sis?" she asked.

"Wes didn't go and pick up the kids, so now I'm gonna have to go and get them."

"Oh no."

"I know. Now, my night is going to end early because of his stupid ass."

She said, "It's ok sis. We don't have to go out."

"Yes we do. You're in town. I never get to see you anymore, and I never get out anymore. I needed this tonight."

"I know, but it's ok." she said.

"No, it's really not. I'm tired of his shit girl. He can't do one simple thing right." I said as I called my mom back.

When she answered, I said, "Hey mom. I'm sorry. I don't know where Wes is. I called him twice and he is not answering. I'll come and get the kids now."

"No. That's ok daughter. Have fun. I'll reschedule what I had to do. They are asleep anyway. No need to rush and wake them up. They are fine with me."

"Mom, are you sure?"

"Yes chile, go and have fun. I'll see you tomorrow."

"Ok. Thank you so much mom."

"No problem."

"Girl I could punch him right now." I said when I hung up with my mom. I put my phone into my purse and said, "I know he's probably with his other baby momma who he claims that he ain't messing with. He thinks that I'm stupid, but I'm not stupid." I said as I zipped up my handbag.

"I don't even know why you put up with that mess." she said.

"I don't know either. Mainly because I was trying to give it a chance for my kids and because he was acting like he was going to do right this time. I don't know if I can do it anymore though. He was doing good at first, but now he is back up to the same old shit. I got two kids by him now. Ugh. Sometimes I wish I could just take back the day I conceived Aiden. I was doing fine without him. Now, all he is doing is bringing stress back into my life. I'm over it."

"I understand sis. Well, I'm here for you, if you need me."

"Thanks sis."

"Always."

"I miss you."

"I miss you too."

"That's enough about me. Are you sure everything is alright with you?"

"Yes everything is fine." she said as she smoothed down the back of her short haircut. I was happy to see that she was still rocking the short hair. It looked good on her.

"Ok if you say so." I said as we turned to walk back to the table where Nikita and Kyra were finishing their meals. "That haircut still looks good on you too." I said.

"Thank you." she replied.

"You should let me touch it up while you're here."

"Of course sis. You know that I wasn't going to leave without letting you get in this hair."

"How are those stylists out east treating you anyways?"

"I mean they're cool, but they're not you sis. I miss you in my hair girl. Nobody does it like you."

I smiled and flicked my long black tresses off my shoulder. As I was looking at Chanel's hair, I noticed a bruise on her shoulder.

My eyebrows crumpled, and then I asked, "Sis is that bruise on your shoulder?"

"Huh? Where?" Chanel asked.

"Right here." I said as he pointed to the large black and purple circle her shoulder.

"Oh yea. I forgot that was there. I bumped into the corner of my dresser." Chanel said.

"The corner of the dresser?" I asked.

"Yes I tripped over something in my room. I didn't know that I bruised up."

"Hmm ok." I said. Something about what my sister was saying didn't sound right but I chose not to press her about it.

"What's up cousin?" Nikita asked when we approached the table.

"Girl, dumb ass didn't pick up the kids." I said.

"So, we not going out?" Nikita asked.

"Yes we are. My mom decided to keep them until tomorrow for me so I can have some fun."

Kyra said, "Aww that was nice of her."

"Yea I love my mom." I said.

"Ok good. Because this will be my last turn up for a while. After I drop this baby, I'm going to be tied down for a while." Nikita said.

"I know, so y'all ready?" I asked.

"Yes." Kyra said as she threw her napkin into her empty plate. "We've got to come here again this food was amazing."

"For sure. This is my sis's favorite spot."

"Sure is." Chanel said as she looked down at her phone. She put her phone into her purse, as the waitress took my card to pay for the bill. After she came back with the receipt for me to sign, we left the restaurant and headed to the club.

Chapter 16

Chanel

Keep fucking playing with me.

I read the text again before putting my phone into my clutch purse. It was the last text Orlando had sent to me thirty minutes prior to me reading it again. I didn't respond. I wasn't going to put up with his craziness that night. I was home with my family and friends, and I planned to have fun whether he liked it or not. If Orlando didn't calm down, I was prepared to ask Adara if I could spend the night at her house. After that last text he had gone quiet, so I was hoping he had hooked up with his friends and gone out somewhere.

We parked and walked to the nightclub. There was a long line outside of the club full of patrons eager to get in, drink, and party the night away. I know that I was ready to party the night away. I hadn't had fun in a long time. I hadn't laughed, or even so much as felt happy in a long time. The only time I got out was with the other football wives, and Orlando had pretty much put a stop to that. Every time I planned to go hang out with them, he would fuss, or come up with some reason why he didn't like me to be with them, or he would just hit me enough to bust my lip or black my eye so I couldn't go. Lisa and the girls had even started calling me to see why I hadn't been around in a while. I always gave them some kind of excuse, and then I would promise them that they would see me soon.

I looked around at the scene in the downtown area. There were people scattered everywhere walking to and from nightclubs that lined the block. There were three nightclubs on the block that we were on, and three others on the next block over. Different types of music was bumping out of each club. The one next to us had reggae playing. The one next to that had a mixture of top forty hits blaring from its speakers. The one we were heading towards had a mixture of Rap and RnB music thumping. I started lip syncing the words to one of the songs, when Kyra broke our silence.

"My man is Djing here tonight. I can get us into VIP." Kyra said.

"Oh really!?" Nikita exclaimed.

"Yup. I know security." Kyra said.

"Oh, that's cool. Thank you, girl." Adara said.

"You're welcome."

"Damn look at the line outside of the club. There is a line for VIP too." Nikita said.

"It's always packed here." Kyra said as we walked up.

"I've never been here, but I've heard good things about it." Adara said.

Kyra said, "Yea, it's different now since it is being run by new owners. It's way better. Definitely classier than it used to be. Bianca and Deon come down here a lot. We might see them tonight."

We were standing in the back of the VIP line swaying and bopping to the music playing inside of the club; patiently waiting to get inside of the club so we could party. Nikita reached into her purse and pulled out a large flask covered in pink rhinestones out of her purse and said, "I can't drink, but y'all can."

"What the hell?" Adara asked.

Nikita laughed and said, "What cousin?"

"Why do you have a liquor in your purse?" Adara asked.

"I hope you haven't been drinking while pregnant." Kyra said.

Nikita giggled and said, "Hell nah. I have a bottle of liquor because this is how I do it. I figured I'd hook y'all up since I can't drink."

"Leave it up to Nikita to do something ghetto like that." I said.

"Ghetto or not, this is going to get you right, so you're not spending a bunch of money on these overpriced, watered down drinks in the club just to get a buzz."

"I can feel it." Kyra said.

"Ok then, so who's drinking first?" Nikita asked.

"What is it?"

"Vodka. Cîroc. You know how I do."

"You couldn't have at least had some Patron in there?" I asked.

Nikita rolled her eyes at me and asked, "So who's drinking?"

"Alright. I'll go first. Give me that bottle." Adara said.

Adara took a big gulp of the clear liquor, and then she frowned as she felt the burning sensation in her throat and chest. "Woo!" she said after she swallowed the clear liquid. She handed the bottle to me, but I shook my head.

"Girl I don't drink liquor out of a bottle." I said.

"Girl come on. Let loose a little. You're home so have fun." Adara said.

"Yea girl. You don't know when you'll be back here to see us." Nikita said.

I sucked my teeth and then I said, "Alright." I grabbed the hot pink bedazzled flask from Adara and turned it up. I took a huge gulp, and then I handed the bottle to Kyra. The ladies cheered and clapped their hands.

"Whatever." I managed to say after I suffered through the bitter taste of alcohol and the burning sensation as it went down.

"I don't drink much, but I'm doing this for y'all." Kyra said before taking a swig from the bottle, and then she handed the bottle back to Nikita.

"Now y'all about to be right!" Nikita chuckled as she tossed the empty flask back into her purse just as we approached the front of the line.

"Hey Kyra. Good to see you." The security guard said.

"Hey! nice to see you too." she responded.

"All these beautiful ladies with you?"

"Yes they are." Kyra said.

"Cool." the security guard said, and then he opened the velvet rope to let us through.

A pretty lady walked us to a booth in the VIP area. Kyra thanked her, and then we ordered drinks from a waitress who was working the VIP section. After getting drinks, we made our way through the packed club to see who was in there. We stopped to talk to a few people we knew, and then we bumped into Deon and Bianca.

"Hey!" Bianca and Deon yelled over the music.

"Hey y'all!" Adara said.

Everyone hugged, and then Bianca said, "I can't believe you're out Adara. You never come out with me."

"I know, but I had to come out with my sister." Adara said.

"Oh yea! Welcome back!" Bianca said to me.

"Thank you!" I said.

"You two are hanging with us, right? I got us a VIP booth over there." Kyra said.

"Hell yea!" Bianca said.

"Good! I'll be right back." Kyra said. She walked over to the DJ booth to speak to her boyfriend.

The rest of us made our way to the dance floor. After Kyra talked to her boyfriend, she met us on the dance floor. We let the alcohol take control and we turned up. A group of guys who were also on the dance floor started dancing with us. I was having so much fun that I wasn't even thinking about Orlando anymore. I felt carefree, happy, and not worried about the consequences of me ignoring Orlando's angry calls and texts. The guy dancing behind me was cute and had my attention. Kyra's boyfriend was spinning all latest hits and we danced for a while. We dance until Bianca's said her feet were hurting and she needed to sit down, so all of us said goodbye to the guys who were dancing with us, and then we made our way back to the VIP booth to rest. We sat down and watched the rest of the nightclub party, drank, and cracked jokes until the lights turned on. Kyra's boyfriend walked over to us, kissed Kyra on the cheek, spoke to the rest us, and then he thanked us for coming. I was surprised Kyra's boyfriend was a white guy, and he was fine too. He asked Kyra if she was coming with him. Kyra told him that she was, and then asked us if we wanted to go too.

"Where are we going?" Nikita asked.

"It's just a little after set that I do." Kyra's boyfriend said.

"Y'all want to go?" Adara asked.

Everyone said they were down to go, so Kyra said, "Alright I'll meet y'all there. I'm gonna text the address. "

Kyra followed her boyfriend to the DJ booth, and then the rest of us headed out of the club. A girl that was walking out of the at the same time as we were spoke to me.

"Hey, don't I know you from somewhere?" the girl asked.

"I don't know." I said.

"Wait, your Orlando King's wife, right?"

"Yes I am." I said.

"Oh wow! It's great to meet you. I follow you on social media."

"Oh ok. It' good to meet you too." I said.

"You're even more beautiful in person." the girl said.

"Thank you."

"You're so lucky to be married to Orlando. I wish it were me."

"Thank you."

"Looked like you had fun in there."

"I did."

"That's good. Everyone needs to have fun sometimes. Well, have a good night. It was great to meet you."

"Thank you. It was good to meet you too." I said as I watched her walk away.

"Aww you have fans." Nikita said.

"I know. That's crazy." I said.

"That was nice of her to recognize you and say something." Adara said as we stepped out onto the sidewalk.

We looked around at all the people standing outside either talking or making their way to their cars parked in the large parking ramps across the street. The guys we'd met inside stepped outside a couple of minutes after we did and sparked up conversation. Suddenly, everyone heard a car horn beeping and someone yelling my name. Everyone turned their heads and saw Orlando pulling up to the club in an expensive car.

BEEP BEEP

"Chanel!" Orlando yelled.

I turned and looked at him. I exhaled, rolled my eyes, and turned towards Adara.

"Oh my God." I whispered.

"What is he doing here?" Adara asked.

"I don't know." I said, and then I sighed. "I guess this is goodbye. I've got to go."

"Awww girl. I wanted to party some more." Adara said.

"I know."

BEEP BEEP

"Chanel! Let's go!" Orlando yelled.

"Who's that?" the guy I was dancing with asked.

"That is my husband."

"Isn't that Orlando King?" the other guy asked.

"Yes."

"Wow. You're married to Orlando King? Damn girl you're rolling in dough." the guy I danced with said.

BEEP BEEP

"CHANEL!"

I sighed and said, "Let me go before his head pops off. He is already making a scene."

"Alright sis." Adara said in a disappointed tone.

"I'll call you tomorrow so we can hang out some more ok?" I said as I hugged Adara.

"Ok. Well, text me when you guys make it back to the hotel." she said.

"Ok." I said, and then I hugged Nikita, Bianca, and Deon.

BEEP BEEP

"I'm coming!" I yelled at the car as I made my way to it.

I walked up to the car with attitude in my step and snatched the door open. I got into the car, and Orlando sped off down the street.

Orlando smacked me in the back of the head and then he yelled, "What the fuck is your problem!"

I grabbed my head and began to cry. I yelled, "Stop Orlando!"

"Oh stop now, right!? Why the fuck do I have to come and find my wife at a fucking club!?"

"How did you even know where I was!?"

"Don't worry about how I know! You tell me why the fuck you were standing outside with a bunch of dudes and why the fuck were you dancing on dudes up in the club!?"

"Huh!?"

"Don't act fucking stupid! You know what the fuck I'm talking about!" Orlando yelled, and then he hit me again.

"I wasn't dancing with nobody!" I lied.

"Oh you lying now!? You don't know what the fuck I'm talking about!?" Orlando yelled. Orlando picked up his phone swiped the screen to open it up, and then dropped the phone in my lap. "Look at that shit!" Orlando yelled.

I looked down at the phone and saw a short video clip of me in the club dancing on the guy I was standing outside with. The girl that spoke to me in the club had sent him the video clip via social media. I immediately recognized her face in the profile pic next to the message.

Oh my God. That dumb bitch. I thought.

Orlando grabbed me by my head and yelled, "What the fuck is that shit! Huh!?"

"I don't know! I was just having fun Orlando!" I said as I held the back of my head with tears streaming down my face. I wished in that moment I could go back, see that girl in the club, and smack the mess out of her for smiling in my face, being fake nice, and then sending Orlando that video. *I'm getting my ass beat because of that dumb bitch.* I thought.

"That's what you call having fun!?" he pushed my head into the window hard.

My head smacked glass, and then she screamed, "I was just dancing! Orlando stop!"

"You want me to stop!? Alright, I'ma stop. Just wait 'til we get back to the room." Orlando said as he cracked his knuckles.

I kept my body leaning against the passenger door. I had my head down crying into my hands. I couldn't even imagine what was in store for me once we got back to the hotel room. Part of me wanted to jump out of the car while it was moving. I figured the injuries that I would sustain from the leap wouldn't be any worse than what Orlando was going to do to me.

I also thought about jumping out the car and running when we got to the hotel, but I thought about how much worse the beating might be if he caught up to me. I hoped that the Percocet pill that I'd taken hours earlier might help with what I was about to go through.

Orlando was silent the rest of the ride. He pulled up to Valet parking and told me to get out of the car. I got out and kept my head down as I walked into the hotel. Orlando gave the keys to the valet driver, and then he followed behind me in silence. I listened to the elevator beep as it went up each floor to the top level where the presidential suites were. Each beep was a reminder of how much closer I was getting to the nightmare that was about to happen. I started to regret not sending him my location, or responding to him, or even going out with my girls in the first place.

We reached the top floor and he followed me to the door to our suite. As soon as I heard the door closed behind us, he grabbed me by the back of my neck and began to savagely beat me.

Chapter 17

Adara

All of us looked at each other when Chanel walked away. I didn't like it. I didn't like it at all. Everyone was shocked at how he was acting. I was pissed at how he was acting. I didn't like the way he was yelling at my sister like he was. Nothing about it sat well with me.

"Damn he was tripping cousin." Nikita said.

"Yes he really was. That's why I can't stand his lame ass. I don't even know why she married him." I said.

"Yea girl. He was yelling like he was talking to his child or something. It couldn't be me." Deon said.

"What was that about girl?" Bianca asked.

"I don't know, but I'm going to find out." I said.

"Girl you should check on your God sis. That dude is crazy." Deon said.

I agreed with him. After seeing that huge bruise on her back, and then witnessing his behavior that night, I was for sure something was going on behind closed doors that Chanel was hiding. I wasn't buying her excuse for the reason she had the bruise either.

"Fuck it. Y'all ready to go?" Deon asked.

"Yea." I said.

"Good cause I'm ready to drink some more." Deon said.

"Ok!" Bianca yelled.

"Nikita tapped me and asked, "Are you sure that you still want to go?"

"Yea. Kyra is waiting for us."

"Ok." Nikita said, and then we began walking towards the parking garage.

"That was crazy cousin. What do you think about it?" Nikita asked me as we were walking through the ramp towards my car.

"I don't like it, and you know that I have never liked him. It was crazy how he pulled up, and then all that beeping the horn and yelling was even crazier. He was yelling like he owns her or something."

Nikita said, "Yea, and did you see how she looked when she walked away?"

I said, "Yea, like a child that was in trouble."

"Are you going to talk to her about it?" she asked.

"I plan to." I said as we got into my car. I started the engine and backed out of the parking spot. "I noticed a bruise on her back today. I hope he's not putting his hands on my sister." I said as I pulled out of the parking garage into traffic.

"Yea, I noticed that too. I wasn't gonna say anything." Nikita said.

"I asked her about it, and she gave me some bogus ass excuse like she ran into something. It just doesn't sound right."

"Nah. That sounds like some bullshit cousin."

"Right."

"I know she a gold digger and all, but would she take an ass beating for money?"

"Cousin."

"I'm just saying."

"I know. I don't know. I hope not. I hope she would be smart enough to get out of a situation like that, if that *is* what *is* going on."

"I know me and her don't always get along, but I'm not ok with any man putting his hands on any woman. We can beat his ass if you want to."

I chuckled a little and asked, "What are you gonna do with your belly in the way?"

"Shit you know I got hands. Pregnant and all. I used to fight my brothers all the time."

"I'll give it to you. You do got hands though. I've seen you whoop a few asses before."

"Yup. I'm not a joke."

I chuckled and said, "Well, I'm going to investigate a little before we jump the gun. Plus we're ladies. We don't need to fight a man, but we can call your brothers to put a foot in his bitch ass." I said as I pulled into the parking lot of the building the after set was being held in. Deon and Bianca pulled into the parking lot right behind us.

We parked, got out of our cars, and walked into the building. The place looked like an old warehouse converted into a low key, underground, nightclub. It was very dark with a mixture of weed, cigarette, and hookah smoke clouding the air. There were a bunch of people from the club in there.

Corey who goes by the name DJ C Sizzle was spinning some popular reggae and dance hall songs. There were a bunch of people dancing in the middle of the warehouse. The people who just liked to smoke and observe had most of the seats filled. There were also people lining the walls. Deon and Bianca spotted some people that they knew and stopped to smoke. Nikita and I were checking out everyone as we continued to walk through the club.

Kyra spotted us, walked up and said, "Hey ladies! Thanks for coming!"

"Hey girl! You're welcome. How long does this go until?" I asked.

"Four or sometimes five in the morning depending on the crowd."

"People be in here until five in the morning?" I asked.

"Girl, yes." she said, and then she asked me, "Where is Chanel?"

"Her husband showed up, so she had to go home."

"Oh ok. Well, do you want a drink?"

"Sure. I can use one."

"Alright. Come on."

Nikita and I followed her through the dark club to the bar. While Kyra was ordering the drinks, I turned around so I can view of the club from the bar. I wanted to see who was in there. I scanned the club. I saw a few cute guys, some under dressed females, a couple of people I knew from school, a few of my clients, and then my eyes stopped.

I knew it wasn't who I thought it was. I knew my eyes had to be deceiving me, but they weren't. I saw my baby's father standing up against the wall with a blunt in his mouth some hood rat looking chick twerking on him with some little ass shorts on and her butt hanging out the bottom.

I said, "Oh hell no."

"What?" Nikita asked.

"Look at who has his ass up in here instead of at home with our kids." I said angrily.

Nikita turned around, scanned the club, and spotted him."

"Oh wow. So, this is why he forgot to pick up the kids? And who is that bitch twerking all on him?"

"I don't know, but I'm about to find out." I said furiously.

Before Kyra could turn around and acknowledge what was happening, Nikita and I had quickly b-lined across the warehouse club to Wes.

"Uh. What the fuck are you doing?" I asked when I stepped to him. I asked the question with force and a lot of attitude. He knew I was pissed. His eyes were so glued on the chicks ass that he didn't even see us coming. My question startled him. The girl stopped dancing on him and stepped back when she saw me and Nikita.

"Adara? Fuck are you doing here?" he asked.

"I'm asking you the same thing, and who the fuck is this?" I asked as Nikita eye balled the girl. The girl took the hint and walked away.

"Why y'all walking up on me like that? Like y'all the police or something?" Wes asked.

"I'm waiting for you to explained why you're up in here with this chick, not answering my phone calls, and not at home with our kids?"

"Look, I'm a grown man. Don't talk to me like I'm a child. Get up out my face with that bullshit."

When I heard him say, get up out my face, I snapped. I pointed my finger in his face, and yelled, "Get up out your face!? You supposed to be at home with our kids, but you're up in here with that bitch!? You would rather be around some scattered hoe's ass but not your kids! Fuck you Wes!"

Wes pushed my finger out of his face and that pushed me over the edge. I balled my hand up into a fist and started to swing. I don't know what made me feel like I could fight a man, but I was so pissed and tipsy that I just wanted to beat him up. Nikita grabbed me and Kyra ran over to help pull me away from him. His friends stepped in and pulled him away from me.

"You gonna hit me Adara? Really?" he yelled.

"You damn right!" I yelled.

"Let's go cousin." Nikita said to me as she and Kyra pushed me towards the door.

"He got me so fucked up!" I yelled.

Deon and Bianca saw the commotion and ran over to help. "Girl what happened?" she asked as her and Deon followed us out of the door.

"Wes's stupid ass!" I yelled.

"He's here?" Bianca asked as we stepped out onto the sidewalk.

"Yes!" I yelled. I was still extremely mad.

"He was dancing with some thot looking ass girl." Nikita said.

"Oh boy." Deon said.

"I could have socked his ass in his mouth!" I yelled.

"Cousin calm down." Nikita said.

"Yea girl, don't let that shit work you up." Bianca said.

Kyra had her hands on my shoulders slowly squeezing them to help me calm down. I took a few deep breaths to try to get myself under control. Wes and his friends exited the club a few minutes later. Wes walked over to me to try to talk to me, but all my friends stepped in front of me to block him from me.

"Adara can I talk to you for a second?"

"Leave me alone Wes!"

"So, you're going to let your girl gang stop me from talking to you?" he asked.

"Look, she said that she doesn't want to be bothered with you, so go on." Deon said.

"Look, man I ain't talking to you."

"Leave me the fuck alone Wes!" I yelled again. "Go find that bitch you were dancing with!"

"She said go, now bye." Deon said.

"Dude I'll beat your mutha fucking ass."

"Try me." Deon said.

"Punk ass dude!" Wes said as he walked towards Deon, but Wes's friends grabbed him. "Let's go bro. It ain't even worth it." one of his friends said.

"You lucky." he said to Deon before turning to walk away.

"Come on girl. Let's go." Nikita said after Wes and his friends got into their car.

"I'm sorry Kyra." I said.

Kyra said, "No. It's fine. Go home. Text me to let me know you made it."

"I will." All of us hugged each other, and then Nikita and I left.

Chapter 18

Adara

Nikita got into her car and went home when we made it back to my house. I took a bath, put on my pajamas, and laid down to go to sleep. At least I attempted to go to sleep, but I couldn't relax because I was still extremely upset with Wes. I wound up lying on my back staring at the ceiling for a while, and then I picked up my phone and scrolled through my social media timeline for a while. When I finally felt relaxed enough to go to sleep, I put my phone down and turned over to my side.

I was just about to fall into a good snooze when I heard Wes's keys in the door. It was a little after five o'clock in the morning. I heard him walk in and decided to lay there and play like I was asleep so he wouldn't bother me. I hoped that he would pass out on the couch, but nope, not Wes. He walked right into the bedroom and climbed right on top of me.

"Adara." he whispered.

I stayed silent.

"What the fuck is your problem? Huh?" he whispered.

I didn't respond.

"Stop trying to play like your sleep. I know you're up."

I sighed and said, "Get off me Wes."

"No. Why you come up in the club tripping? Mobbing up on me with your cousin like y'all were about to jump me?"

"Wes move." I said as I pushed him off me and sat up in the bed. I could smell liquor on his breath, and it was irritating me and making me nauseous.

"I'm trying to talk to you."

"You want to talk to me now Wes after not answering my many phone calls?"

"I didn't know that you called."

"You forgot the kids Wes!" I yelled.

"Adara please don't start yelling."

"How do you forget your own kids!?"

"I did and I'm sorry."

"Sorry is not going to cut it."

"I don't know what you want me to do or say."

"Then to run into you at a club all over some bitch!"

"I wasn't all over her. She was dancing on me."

"She had her big, sloppy ass all over your dick!"

"Adara quit yelling."

"How can I not yell! I just caught my man in the club dancing with some hoe!"

"Ok, but you didn't have to come over there tripping like that."

"Why didn't I? I just saw my man, my child's father in the club dancing with some ratchet ass bitch and I'm not supposed to say anything! Why the hell were you dancing on her like that and you have a woman at home!?"

"Adara, she started dancing on me."

"Why didn't you stop her?"

"I don't know."

"So you're out here acting single?"

"No. I'm not."

"That's not what it looked like to me Wes!"

"I don't know what it look like to you, but that's not what it was. It was just a dance."

"It was just a dance? So, I can go out and let a dude dance on me then."

"If you want to get his ass beat."

"Alright then, but it's ok for you. Nah. It's not!"

"Alright Adara, baby, I'm sorry. It won't happen again. Would you please calm down." he said as he climbed back on top of me.

"Move Wes." I said.

"I apologize baby ok."

"No because you think that you can just apologize and it's over." I said. He leaned to try to kiss me, but I put my hand up to block him.

"Leave me alone and get out."

He tried to kiss me again, but I moved my face and yelled, "Move Wes! Leave me alone! Get out!"

"No. I'm not going nowhere."

"Fine." I said, and then I pushed him off me again, threw the cover off me, grabbed a pillow, and stormed out of the bedroom.

"Adara." he called after me.

"No! And your breath stinks! You smell like a liquor store!"

"Shut up. You've been drinking too so you're not innocent."

I didn't respond. I didn't feel like addressing the fact that he'd been drinking. I'd had enough of him that night and I just needed space and wanted to be left alone. I slammed my pillow down on the couch, walked to the hall closet to pull out my guest blanket, and then I laid down for my second time sleeping on the couch because of him. He didn't follow me into the living room. He stayed in the bedroom and passed out in the bed with all his clothes on.

Chapter 19

Kyra

The moment she saw Corey that night, she knew that he was high. His movements and the way he was talking told her immediately. Part of her resented that he had went out on the last tour. It was a blessing because they needed the money, but it was a curse because it resurrected old demons that she wasn't ready to face again. She noticed the signs of him being under the influence that night when she walked up on the stage to give him a hug and kiss.

"Hey baby. What's up? What's Up!?" he asked excitedly as he started looking for the next song to play in his computer. He was talking fast like he did every time he was under the influence. his mood also seemed extra happy and hyped and Kyra knew her man. Corey was never that turned up without an enhancement. Kyra's man was a mellow kind of fellow.

When Corey found the song that he was looking for, he mixed it into the song that he was playing on the mixing board, and then he watched the crowd go crazy and start cheering and singing along. That was the part he loved the most about his job. Making people happy and watching them party. He said a few words in the mic giving his girl a shout out and a few of his friends, and then he took his headset off. Corey turned to hug Kyra, and then he kissed her on the lips. Kyra looked into his eyes before hugging him and noticed how glossy they were. She was all too familiar with that look.

"Hi baby." she said, looking him directly in the eyes.

"You want a drink baby? I got you. Let's get you a drink." he said quickly.

"No baby. I'm ok. I'm with my girls in VIP. We already got drinks."

"Ok. Ok. Well, if y'all need something just let me know. Ok?" he said.

"Alright." Kyra said. She decided not to address the obvious right then while he was at work.

Oh lord. she thought as she made her way back to the dance floor where Adara and everyone else was. She blended in with the party and began to dance with everyone. Even though she was dancing and laughing with them, she couldn't help but to be in her thoughts. *I hope he doesn't get on it bad again like he was the last time.* she thought.

Kyra thought about how he had spent up his money he made on the last couple of tours on drugs and she ended up having to take care of everything for a long time. The little bit that he was making from local clubs wasn't enough. Every time he found a regular job, he found a way to either quit or get fired. His excuse was that it wasn't his passion. Kyra would argue that he was delusional, and he needed to get a reality check, but Corey would assure her that he was following his dreams and doing that would bring him some real money. It did when he would get a bunch of gigs back to back on the road, but times had changed.

When he was younger, he was in high demand. He was one of the highest paid DJ's. That was when life was good for them. Before his drug habit got bad and people caught wind of it. People didn't want to deal with him because he was a liability. Especially after he passed out in a club one night at a celebrity function, and then another time backstage at a show. His high demand status was drying up and it didn't help that there were so many new and young social media DJ's coming up, and ready to work. They were stealing all the gigs is what Corey would complain to Kyra about every time he didn't get a call about a job he wanted.

Corey lucked up and got a call from a friend who was going back out on tour. Although Kyra didn't want him to go, she knew that it was what he ultimately wanted. It was the opportunity he needed that could possibly open more doors, and she couldn't pull herself to try to take that away from him. Plus they needed the money badly, so she told him that she was alright with him going as long as he promised not to pick up his drug habit again. He had just gotten clean a few months prior. Kyra knew that it wasn't enough time for Corey to be around that temptation again. Corey promised that he was alright and could handle it, but the demon they had fought prior to Corey going was showing back up.

I don't want to go through this again. she thought.

Kyra remembered the nights that he wouldn't sleep. Sometimes he would be up for days. She remembered the nights she couldn't find him, or the nights he would leave in the middle of the night to get a bag. It didn't matter how much she fussed, cried, or threatened to end the relationship, he would not stop. Kyra couldn't win. It felt like a battle that she would never win, and then she finally convinced him to go to treatment to get clean after years of fighting with him. Right after he finished treatment, he got the job to go on tour. Corey jumped at the chance, and Kyra was just as happy to see him happy.

When the club night was over, Corey made his way through the club to Kyra and her friends.

"Hey sexy." he said when he walked up, and then he sniffled.

Ugh. she thought. There was that sniffle again. Anytime he was using, he had a constant nasal drip like he had a never-ending sinus infection or head cold.

"Hey." Kyra replied giving him direct eye contact. It was her way of telling him that she was aware of what was going on. Corey picked up on her silent communication but ignored it.

"You ready to go?" he asked Kyra.

"Yes" Kyra said.

She turned to her friends and asked, "Y'all coming?"

"Where?" Nikita asked.

"To this little after set I do." Corey said.

"Yea we're coming." Nikita said.

"Alright. Kyra will text y'all the address. See you there." he said before taking Kyra by the hand and walking with her back through the club. After he packed up his DJ equipment, Kyra followed him out of the back door of the club to his car. Kyra opened the car door and got in. Corey go into the car on the driver's side.

"Did you have fun tonight?" he asked as he pulled his seatbelt on.

Kyra pulled her seatbelt on, and then she said, "I did."

Corey sniffled and said, "Good. I'm glad."

"Are you high Corey?" she asked.

"No." Corey said.

"Corey."

"What?"

"Don't lie."

"Look, stop asking me that. I told you I'm not. Now, can we quit talking about it? Damn." he said angrily.

"Alright. Fine. I hope you're not because I'm not going through this shit again."

"You've already said that."

"I'm going to keep saying it."

"I don't need you to keep repeating the same thing over and over again Kyra. I hate when you do that. I heard you the first time."

They were silent for a moment, and then Kyra said, "I see that girl was here tonight."

"Who?"

"You know who. You're little friend that you like to get high with."

"Oh yea. I didn't invite her. She just came to support I guess."

"You better not be cheating on me again with her Corey. I already told you."

"I know. If I cheat again, it's over."

"Especially if you do it with her."

"I know."

"I'm serious."

"Kyra, baby, I'm not using. I'm not cheating. I don't know why she was there. End of story. Ok?"

Kyra sighed and replied, "Ok."

Years prior, Corey was running around with a blonde hair, blue eyed, white girl named Tasi. She was a stripper that liked to snort cocaine too. They had been cheating for almost a year before Kyra found out. Corey got Tasi pregnant. Tasi got mad at Corey and told Kyra, but she lost the baby.

Kyra was beyond upset when she found out about the pregnancy. She constantly threw it in his face during arguments and threatened to leave. Part of her was relieved when she found out that Tasi lost the baby. Corey acted like he didn't care, but Kyra knew that he did. He broke it off with Tasi after her miscarriage and promised Kyra that he would never cheat on her again. She promised Corey that she wouldn't bring it up anymore but seeing Tasi that night triggered her thoughts of distrust. Even though Corey said he didn't know why Tasi was there, Kyra had her suspicions.

Chapter 20

Kyra

Kyra made her way through her house straitening things, lighting candles, burning sage, and humming to one of her favorite Music Soulchild songs. She was waiting for her bestfriend to arrive. She had just flew in from Atlanta. Kyra was excited to see her bestfriend. She hadn't seen her in six months.

Kyra smiled when she heard the doorbell. She jogged to the door and snatched it open.

"Hey lady!" she said, and then they embraced for a moment before Kyra pulled her inside of the house and closed the door.

"I'm so happy to see you!" Destiny said.

"I'm happy to see you too."

"I wish I would have come during the summer. It's chilly."

"Yea I know. This is considered spring."

"This is not spring. It is hot as fuck down south right now." Destiny said as she followed Kyra through the house.

"I know. Be glad you're not here during the winter." Kyra said, and then she pulled a chair out at the dining room table so Destiny could sit down.

"I don't have time for that winter mess y'all go through up here. I'm glad I'll be out of here way before that."

Kyra pulled a chair out across the table from Destiny, sat down, and then she said, "I wish I was getting out of here before that."

"I told you to come down to Atlanta with me." Destiny said.

"Girl I can't pack up and move to Atlanta."

"Why not?"

"Because I can't leave my house. You hungry? I made some Salmon croquets and red beans and rice."

"Yes I'm starving."

"Ok let me make you a plate." Kyra said as she stood up and headed towards the kitchen. Destiny continued talking while she watched her friend walk to the kitchen to make her a plate of food.

"Girl you don't have nothing up here, but Corey and this house. You can sell this house or rent it, make a profit, and start over somewhere else. You'll probably build a better clientele down there anyways."

Kyra walked back into the dining room with a plate of steaming food. She said, "You always say that. White or red?"

"Red."

"Merlot, Cabernet Sauvignon, or Pinot Noir?"

"Pinot is good."

"Alright." Kyra said and walked back to the kitchen.

"Girl I'm telling you. You'll be happier there."

"I don't know." Kyra said as she walked back into the dining room with two glasses of red wine. She handed Destiny a glass, and then she sat down. She took a sip and set the glass on the table.

Destiny took a sip of her wine, set the glass on the table, and then said, "You really don't have family here, but you will have me and my family down there and you know we love you." She picked up her fork and took a bite off food.

"I know."

"Well what are you waiting for? Corey to keep fucking up?"

Kyra shrugged her shoulders and took another sip of her wine. Destiny took that as a que to change the subject.

"Girl this food is amazing per usual. You need to open a restaurant."

"I don't want to cook for a living. I just enjoy cooking for my loved ones."

"You never know. You would make a killing."

"Maybe, but I would hate my life." Kyra said.

Destiny chuckled and then she asked, "So where are we going tonight?"

"Well, I feel like dancing, so I was thinking about going to Corey's event."

"Where is it?"

"At this club downtown."

"Is it going to be ratchet and hood?"

"No. You know Corey doesn't do ratchet events."

"Ok cool. Because I am not in the mood to be running or ducking for cover because someone is either fighting or shooting."

"Corey doesn't like that atmosphere. You know he got hit in the head with a bottle once at a hood club when a fight broke out. He said never again after that."

"I remember that. A shame. Speaking of Corey, how has he been?" Destiny asked after taking another sip of wine.

Kyra sighed and then she said, "I think he is using again."

Kyra was happy that her friend was there. She'd been needing someone to confide in about Corey and Destiny was the only person Kyra could talk to. Destiny was the only person in Kyra's life that knew about Corey's drug addiction and other problems besides his family. Kyra always stayed to herself, so she never had a lot of friends.

She was never really close to her family. Especially after her parents died. Corey was all she had and really all she knew besides Bianca. Kyra met Bianca in beauty school, and they became friends. Bianca was more of a work friend to her, so she never grew extremely close to her. Not close enough to share much of her personal life with her.

Kyra met Destiny at a hair convention in Atlanta and grew close with her over the years. Destiny is the daughter of a famous rapper for a father and famous choreographer for a mother. Kyra was doing a hair show at the convention and Destiny liked her work, so they exchanged information. They went from talking about hair to talking about talking about life and became best friends. Then, Destiny introduced Kyra to her mother, and Destiny's mother became Kyra's first celebrity client. After doing Destiny's mothers hair for a few events, she became they family hairstylist for big events. They would fly her out often. Because of that, she became close with the family and even built a tight bond with Destiny's sister Illaya.

Destiny sighed, put her glass down, and said, "No please don't tell me that."

"Yes. I'm starting to notice those same behaviors."

Destiny shook her head and asked, "I thought he got clean?" She took another bite of food.

"He did before he went on tour with your dad and brother."

Kyra being affiliated with the family is how Destiny's dad Illi-J met Corey. He flew down with her for a huge event the family had to do. Illi-J liked Corey and told him that they were planning a tour soon and would call him. Corey didn't think they were really going to call. He was so used to industry talk. A lot of it was smoke and mirrors. No one in the industry really kept their word, but Illi-J actually called and offered him the job. Corey was ecstatic when he got the call.

"So he came back with a habit again?" Destiny asked.

"Yes he did, but he is lying about it, or in denial, but I know, and I don't want to go through this again."

Kyra started to tear up. Destiny put her glass down, stood up, and walked over to Kyra. She wrapped her arms around her friend and hugged her.

"I'm sorry bestie. Don't cry." Destiny said.

Kyra cried into her shoulder for a moment and then lifted to wipe her tears with the back of her hand. Destiny walked away to find tissue for her friend. She located a box of Kleenex in the living room on the coffee table and carried it back into the dining room where Kyra was sitting. She pulled a couple of tissues out of the box and dabbed Kyra's tears with them.

She handed the tissues to her friend and said, "Listen, you don't have to go through this again. You can leave him. I already told you, you have a place to stay in Atlanta. You don't have to stay here friend. You're alone here, but you got us down there."

"I know, but this is all I know."

"Trust me, you know I know girl, but don't let this man pull you down again. He's got issues that he needs to deal with on his own. That's not a battle that you can win. You almost went broke and lost this house the last time he lost control of his habit."

"I did, and I hear you."

"I don't want to see you go through this again. I just feel so bad that it's because of my dad and brother that pushed him back into that life."

"It's not your fault. You dad and brother don't even use. He made that decision on his own."

"Well, I just want you to know that I'm always here for you for whatever. No matter what you decide to do."

"Thank you, bestie."

"You're welcome." Destiny said, and then she stood up and walked back over to her chair and sat down.

"Do you want to go to Corey's event?" Kyra asked as she wiped her eyes.

"Why not? There isn't anything else popping in this whack ass city."

Kyra laughed and said, "You're right."

"When are you coming to Atlanta to visit?"

"I don't know yet, but I'm due for a vacation."

"Well, my mom has some big event coming up and may need your services. I'm gonna let you know."

"Ok. You know I'll do whatever for your mom. I love her."

"She loves you too. On another note, my sister Illaya is talking about coming up here to visit you."

"Oh wow. I just talked to her the other day."

"She just told me today before I left."

"That's exciting. You know she hates it here. Probably more than you do."

"Destiny laughed and said, "That is true."

"I will have to plan to do something fun while she is here."

"Well, she said that she wants to visit her mother's grave and she wants us to go with her for support."

Kyra's eyebrows went up and she asked, "Oh wow. She's ready to take that step?"

"I guess so. That's what she says."

"Wow. That's big."

"I know."

Both ladies knew that was a big step for Destiny's sister Illaya who lost her mother to drug abuse. Illaya never really talked about real mother much. She was raised by her father Illijah who was known as rapper Illi-J and her stepmother Chelice. Illaya's real mom died of a drug overdose when she was young. Illaya confided in Kyra about her mother after they had grown close. She told Kyra that she never really accepted her mother's death, so she never visited her grave site.

Destiny said, "I think it's time for her to face it. It will probably help her sort out a lot of things in her life. especially the men she chooses to deal with."

Kyra laughed and sipped her drink. Destiny said, "I'm serious. I can't stand any of the guys she has ever brought around the family. There is always something wrong with them. Either they don't have a job, or a car, or a house. It's like she always dealing with someone who is needy, and then she is always weak for them and do whatever they ask."

"That's not good."

"She be doing way too much for these fools. I don't know if it's the absence of her mother in her life or not accepting her mother's death or what. The last dude she was dealing with ran off with her car. We had to get it back for her. The dude she is dealing with now is always asking her for money and to do something for him. I know for a fact she has given him over a thousand dollars that he has not paid back."

"That's crazy."

"I know. She may need some counseling because there is no way and not enough love in the world that is going to make me let a dude use me or take advantage of me."

"Girl, I hear you. I hope she finds a good man."

"I do too."

"Speaking of. When are you going to find you a man?"

"Girl I don't have time for relationships. You know I be having my little boo's."

"Seems to me like you're afraid of falling in love. You've ben single for like six years."

"I'm not afraid. I just don't want to deal with the bullshit, and then I see what you, my sister, and my cousin go through and I'm like uh uh. I'm cool on all that. My life is peaceful just the way it is. I fuck with them, and then drop them when I'm tired or they're not acting right. Life is so much simpler this way."

"Um hum. You can't be single forever bestie."

"Who says I can't."

"Some dude is going to catch your heart and lock your ass down one day."

"If he can catch me. I be running like Forest Gump."

Kyra laughed and said, "Oh my gosh. Anyways. Are you going to visit your cousin Leslie while you are here?"

Destiny sighed and said, "Girl I'm for real, but yes I'm going to see her ratchet ass. I need to see that new baby of hers."

"Yea, my work friend just had her baby too." Kyra said.

"Girl, both of them are stupid for dealing with Wesley in my opinion. He ain't shit and he's never going to be shit."

"You have a point."

"First of all, I don't even know why my cousin is so stuck on him. All they ever did was smoke weed, drink, and fuck. And your friend, I don't even know why she is even dealing with someone like him. She is way too good for him. Period. She got two kids by his raggedy ass? Why? She got so much going on for herself. I really hope she leaves his ass alone."

"Yea. That situation is unfortunate. Sounds like we all have issues when it comes to men."

"Not me because I don't have one." Destiny laughed.

Kyra laughed and said, "You're always running like Forest Gump."

Destiny laughed and said, "Yea because I don't have time for bullshit like I said. You ready to go?"

Destiny laughed again and said, "Yes."

The two ladies finished off the rest of their drinks and headed out for the night.

Chapter 21

Kyra

The nightclub was near empty when Kyra and Destiny arrived. There were a few people by the bar and some near the DJ booth, but not as many people as the two ladies were used to seeing at a club event. Kyra and Destiny walked slowly through the nightclub checking out the scene as they made their way to the DJ booth.

"It's kind of empty in here." Destiny said.

"I know." Kyra agreed.

"I wonder where everybody's at?"

"I don't know."

"See, another reason why you need to come to Atlanta. Actually two reasons. The dumb ass weather and this whack ass club scene."

Destiny laughed and said, "Whatever. Anything is a reason for me to come to Atlanta according to you."

"It is. The South is way better."

"No way. With all those racist, make America great again, red hat wearing people down there?"

"Not in Atlanta. It's like black Hollywood."

"Yea probably in your world because you have famous parents."

"No. Just period. Plus, I hate it up here. It's always so dead." Destiny said as they approached the DJ booth. "Hey Corey!" she waved.

Corey took his headset off and said, "What up ladies!"

Kyra noticed immediately noticed that Corey's nose sounded stuffy and his eyes looked glossy. She looked at Destiny who gave her the look that meant she noticed too.

"Good to see you!" Destiny said as he leaned down to hug both of them.

"I've never seen it so empty in here. Where is everyone?" Kyra asked.

"There was a concert tonight, so we're waiting for everyone to get out of there." he said, and then he sniffled and rubbed his nose. "Let me get y'all a drink." he said as he pulled money out of his pocket and handed it to Kyra. She took the money, cut her eyes at him, and turned to walk away. He grabbed her arm and asked, "Hold up. What was that? What is your problem?"

"You know." she said.

"I know what?"

"You know Corey." she said, and then she turned and walked away.

Once they got a few steps away, Destiny looked at her and said, "Yea, he is definitely using again."

"I know. That makes me so mad." Kyra said as they approached the bar. They ordered drinks, and then Destiny said, "That's not good."

"I know. I'm not even going to stress about it right now. You're here. I just want to enjoy myself tonight." Kyra said as they took their drinks from the bartender.

The two ladies leaned against the bar, so they could check out the entire club scene. A few more people had trickled in, but it was still empty. Destiny pulled out her phone to read a text message.

"One of my brothers friends just text and said to come to his private party. It's lit. A bunch of people from the concert are there. A few celebrities are there too. We should go because this shit is lame." Destiny said.

Kyra laughed and said, "Ok, well, let me say goodbye to Corey."

The two ladies quickly swallowed down their drinks, hugged Corey goodbye, and then headed to the private party.

***

It was at a banquet hall on a back street a few miles from the club they were at. It was packed wall to wall with more than enough beautiful women and handsome men.

Destiny's brother's friend greeted them when they arrived, and then he escorted them to his section. He was a popular up and coming singer who performed at the concert that night.

"What up girl!" he said to Destiny.

"What up! This is my bestie." Destiny said as she pointed to Kyra.

"Hi, I'm Kevin." he said as he extended his hand to shake hers.

Kyra shook his hand and said, "Hi, I'm Kyra."

"Nice to meet you Kyra. You're incredibly beautiful."

"Thank you." Kyra blushed, and then Destiny interrupted. "Ok, enough with the flirting. Geesh." she said.

Kyra giggled, and then he said, "Aw stop hating sis."

While Kevin and Destiny went back and forth about Destiny hating, Kyra gave Kevin a quick onceover. Caramel skin complexion, lots of tattoos from the neck down to his fingertips, and he was dressed in designer clothes from head to toe. Kevin was attractive to her. She wondered if he had a big dick like everyone says black men have, or if he could hit it better than Corey had been doing for all the years, they'd been together. She could tell he lived the Rockstar lifestyle, and that was an automatic turn off for her. She was already dealing with his type and she didn't need another drug addict, cheater in her life.

Kyra quickly shook her thoughts about Kevin when she heard him ask, "What y'all drinking?"

"You already know bro. Patron." Destiny said.

"Alright. I got you." he said, and then he walked away.

Destiny said, "I'm sorry girl. He is such a flirt."

"Oh it's ok. I'm not tripping. He seems cool." Kyra said.

"He is though. You don't know who that is?"

"No."

"Girl for real?"

"I'm serious I don't know who that is." Kyra giggled.

"Oh wow. Girl that is Kevin Starr. He's a huge internet sensation. He sings, and he was discovered on Instagram. Now, he has a hit on the radio, he has millions of followers on social media, and now he is on tour with big stars. He went from the hood to being rich. He got big money now."

"I've never heard of him."

"That's because you don't be on social media like that. That's why you be missing out. Girl I swear you live under a rock."

"I do get on social media sometimes. I'm just not all into it like that."

"I'm gonna need you to come out of that Neo Soul/ Classic Soul realm you live in for just a second and listen to some of this new music out here."

"I do listen to new music. Corey plays it and I hear it at the salon."

"Well Kevin can sing his ass off. I mean he got some serious vocals. Have you ever heard that song Savage Love?"

"I think I heard it once."

"Yea girl, it just hit number one last week. He was just on tour with my dad, brother, and your man. He ain't got no kids and no girl. If you didn't have a man, I'd hook you up, but I'm not going to be the reason that you cheat."

Kyra laughed and said, "I wasn't interested anyway."

"Good, then I don't have to cock block."

"Why haven't you tried to get with him?"

"Because he is like a brother to me."

Kevin walked back up with drinks in hand for the ladies and one for him. "Here you go ladies." he said as he handed them the glasses. "The rest of the bottle is on the table and it's all yours, so make yourself comfortable. Especially you." he made eye contact with Kyra. Kyra smiled, and then looked at the ground.

"That's Corey girl bro." Destiny said.

"Who? DJ C-Sizzle?"

"Yup." Destiny said.

He leaned back and said, "Oooh ok. You're with Corey huh? Wow." He put his hands up and said, "Ok, well, let me back off then."

Destiny and Kyra giggled, and then he said, "Ok, well, let's take these shots real quick." They held their glasses up, and then he said, "To new friends."

After they swallowed down the shot of Tequila, he said, "Have fun."

After that, they danced and drank. A bunch of pics and videos were taken and by the end of the night, Kyra was sitting down watching everyone else party. She couldn't keep her eyes off Kevin, and she didn't know why. Kyra had already told herself that she wasn't interested, but something about him was alluring. She sat and watched Kevin and a few other celebrity guys dancing and singing along to a popular Chris Brown song. Some model type females were up in their faces looking for attention, but Kevin didn't look concerned. When the song ended, she watched him scan the party like he was looking for someone, and then he spotted her sitting down. He smiled when they made eye contact and walked over to her.

"Why are you sitting down?" he asked.

"I got tired and Destiny is over there letting some dude chop her up."

"Yea he all over her. Your feet barking though?"

Kyra laughed and said, "A little bit."

He laughed and said, "Wow, you are too beautiful."

"Thank you." she said.

"So, you're Corey's girl, huh?"

"Yea."

"How long y'all been together?"

"Eight years."

"Damn and y'all not married?"

"No."

"I'm trying to figure out how Corey got a beautiful Queen like you. Like damn. You're fine girl."

"Thank you. I don't know. I guess he just did the right things at the right time."

"Corey a fool. I'm not hating, but Corey don't deserve you. You need somebody like me."

"Oh really?"

"You're damn right. I'm gonna leave it at that. Are you on social media, so I can follow you?"

"I have a page, but I'm not on there a lot."

"Here search your name." he said and handed her his phone.

She put her page information in his phone and then said, "That's me right there."

"Cool follow me back."

"You have over 5 million followers. You don't need my follow."

He laughed and said, "For someone who is not on social media much, you sure know a lot."

"Your sis Destiny told me."

"Oh ok. Well, I'll just follow you then."

"I'll gladly accept the follow."

"Don't be a stranger."

Kyra didn't respond, she just smiled, and then she felt her phone buzz. She unlocked it and saw that she had gotten a text message from Corey's friend that she hated.

Hey Ky, Corey done. He passed out in my back seat. I'm at your house, I can't wake him up and I don't know where his keys are at.

Kyra frowned after reading the text. She knew that meant Corey was wasted and she was probably going to have to deal with him puking everywhere. Another thing Corey did frequently. Drink beyond his limit and get wasted to the point where he couldn't walk.

"Ugh." she said in frustration.

"What's wrong?"

"I gotta go. Corey is wasted and I have to go home. Where is Destiny?"

"Over there talking to my boy."

"Alright." she said as she stood up and adjusted her dress.

"Well, hey, it was great meeting you."

"You too."

"Remember what I said."

"I will." Kyra said, and then she walked quickly over to Destiny. After she told her what was going on, Destiny ended her conversation, and then the ladies left in a hurry.

***

They made it to Kyra's house in fifteen minutes to find Corey passed out in his friends back seat with his shirt off and vomit on his pants.

"I tried to get him up, but he wasn't budging." his friend said.

"Corey!" Kyra called out to him, but he didn't respond. "Corey!" she repeated while shaking him.

He opened his eyes a little, but he passed back out.

"Ugh. I hate when you do this."

"Ky, I can carry him in. I just need you to open the door."

Kyra opened the door, and then the two ladies watched Corey's friend pick him up, put his over his shoulder, carry him into the house, and lay him in the bed. Kyra rolled her eyes at the site of her man passed out yet again.

Destiny turned to her and said, "Ok girl, I'm going to get back to my hotel room and get some rest, but are you good?"

"Yes I'm fine."

"Ok. I'll text you to let you know that I made it there safe, and then I will call you tomorrow."

***

The next morning Corey rolled over in bed and kissed Kyra. She opened her eyes and looked at him.

"You're up now?" Kyra asked.

"Yes."

"You know you were wasted last night, right?"

"Was I?"

"Yes. You were black out drunk. You're friend had to carry you in here."

"I don't remember none of that shit baby. I didn't even know I was home. I don't even know how I got here."

"That's not cool Corey."

"Don't be acting all innocent. You used to get fucked up too when I met you."

"Yea, but how long ago was that Corey? Eight years ago. I've changed since then. What you did last night is dangerous. People die from shit like that. You told me that you were done drinking like that and you were done with drugs before you went out on tour."

"Baby, I was having fun. I just got a little carried away with the drinking."

"No, that is regular behavior for you when your drinking. You don't know your limits. You don't know how to stop. You want to keep going until you black out. You're too old for that now. We're not in our early twenties anymore. I'm not trying to babysit you every time you get like that. I had to get you undressed last night. I don't like how you are when you're drunk like that. You're very mean and you say a lot of things that you don't normally say to me."

Corey looked at Kyra and said, "Alright. I don't want to talk about it anymore. I apologize."

Kyra folded her arms and said, "Fine."

"Let me make it up to you." he said, and then he put his head under the blanket, pushed her legs up and started tongue kissing her peach. Kyra's anger turned to pleasure as his tongue did laps around her pearl. He kissed and licked her thoughts of frustration away, and then Corey climbed on top of her after giving her oral pleasure and put his thick tool inside of her. She wrapped her legs around him and rode his strokes.

"Mmmm Corey!" she moaned when she reached her climax. He pulled out and turned her over onto her stomach. He put his tool back inside of her and gave her short aggressive thrusts while squeezing her firm buttocks, and then he gave her back side a hard smack and made her screech pleasurable sounds.

"Ahhhhhh." she groaned as she felt his thickness fill her up.

"Mmmm baby." he moaned as he felt her release her essence onto him again.

Corey put his hands into Kyra's hair and pulled her head towards him as he continued to thrust in and out of her. He smacked her backside a few more times making her moan his name, and then he busted inside of her. He pulled out and laid next to her. He kissed her a few times on her shoulder, and then Corey got up and went to the bathroom.

Kyra laid there still in a pleasure trance for a moment, and then she sat up. Kyra slid down to the foot of the bed and swung her feet over the foot board. She sat there for a minute trying to motivate herself to get up and make breakfast for her man. Kyra rubbed her hands through her curly hair. She made a mental note to straighten it so she could trim her ends, and then she heard Corey's phone vibrating on the bed. Kyra moved the covers around until she found it. She picked it up and looked at the incoming call. Tasi's name was on the screen. Kyra frowned and answer it.

"Hello?" Kyra said, and but the girl hung up. She jumped out of bed and stormed into the bathroom with the phone in hand.

"What the hell is Tasi doing calling you!" she asked.

Corey looked up from the sink with a mouth full of toothpaste and asked, "What are you talking about?"

"Tasi just called you and she hung up on me! Why is she calling your phone?"

"You answered my phone?"

"Yes I did!"

"Why would you do something like that Ky?"

"Because I did. I wanted to see why she was calling."

"You wrong for that. You dead wrong for that."

"Are you getting high with her again?

"What?"

"Are you snorting coke with her, sleeping with her, and eating her pussy like you used to?"

"I see that you don't get over shit."

"That is what she told me that you were doing with her, so are you doing it again?"

Corey rinsed the toothpaste from his mouth while Kyra waited for an answer. He wiped his mouth with a towel and said, "Look, I don't even know why she called me."

"Well, let's call her now so we can tell her to stop calling." Kyra said

"I'm not doing that."

"Well then you're not doing this with me anymore."

"Kyra stop it. I'm hungry. Will you cook us a meal please?"

"I'm not playing Corey."

"I'm not playing either Kyra. I'm hungry and I have a splitting headache. Now, will you please make us some food. Please baby?" he pleaded.

Kyra folded her arms across again and said, "Fine Cory. Whatever. If I find out you're messing with her again, it's over."

Chapter 22

Chanel

"Look at this shit!" Orlando yelled. "You're all over the blogs!"

He stormed towards me and put his phone in my face. There I was on TMZ in the video that girl secretly recorded of me dancing on a guy in the club.

The headline read: *Orlando Kings Wife's Wild Night. Could she be cheating?*

I looked at the phone and then looked back into the bathroom mirror. I was getting dressed to meet up with

Adara and the girls for my last day in town. Me and Orlando were heading back home the next morning. I'd prayed that nothing else would set Orlando off during the trip. My body was still sore from the last beating and I had to drag myself out of bed just to get ready. I'd popped a couple of pain pills to relieve the pain and forget about what happened. I was just started feeling the effects of those. I just wanted to get dressed and get out of there peacefully with no problems, but there he was yelling about something. What I was going through was not how I imagined my life to be while married to a sports star.

"My wife shaking her ass all in the club is on every blog site and gossip show!" Orlando yelled.

"Orlando, I apologize. I didn't know that I was being recorded." I said as I put eye shadow on my eyes.

"How could you not know? You're Orlando King's wife who shouldn't be shaking her ass with no dude in the club."

"I'm sorry Orlando, but as you can see in the video, he walked up on me while *I* was dancing." I put the eye shadow brush down and picked up my eyeliner pencil.

"And you should have stopped!" he yelled.

"Baby, I was just in the moment. I didn't mean anything by it." I pleaded as I drew black eyeliner across my lower lash line.

"You didn't mean anything by it? You had your ass on another man's dick! Now, I got to deal with my friends and teammates talking shit about me and my wife."

"Well it can't be no worse than you in the blogs kissing some random chick. What do you think was happening to me?" I said as I put the eyeliner pencil down.

"That doesn't have shit to do with this!"

"Oh, so it's ok for you, but not for me."

"So, you think because I got caught up in some bullshit, you're about to be on some bullshit?!"

"No, that's not what I'm saying." I said, and then I blotted powder over my most recent bruise under my eye.

"Yea, that's what the fuck you think." he said, and then he smacked me in the face. The power brush flew out of my hand, and then he grabbed my head and made me look at him. My eyes began to water.

"Play with me if you want to!" he said. "I better not ever see no shit like that again! Do you hear me?"

"Yes Orlando. Please stop." I whimpered.

"As a matter a fact, you're not going nowhere."

"Adara is waiting for me. Please don't ruin this last day."

"I don't give a fuck. You already ruined it with this bullshit." he said, and then he grabbed my shirt, pulled me to the floor, punched me in the chest, and then began dragging me from the bathroom into the room. I screeched when I hit the floor. When I felt the blow from the hit, I grabbed my chest and began to cry out.

"Shut the fuck up!" he yelled, and then he let go of my shirt, climbed on top of me, and wrapped his hands around my neck.

"You don't bite the hand that feeds you bitch! I made you! You ain't shit without me! You don't have shit without me! Where you going to go? Huh? You gonna come back here and live with your momma? You have nothing! You have no life without me! You have no job! You broke and you homeless! Everything you own I got for you so it's mine! Without me you just a regular basic bitch! So don't you ever disrespect me like that again!" he yelled into my face as he squeezed the life out of me.

KNOCK, KNOCK, KNOCK

A sudden knock at the door startled Orlando and stopped him from finishing what he started. He let go of me and walked to the door. I stayed lying on the floor crying and trying to catch my breath. I heard him ask who was at the door. I knew that I could get up and make a run for it, but I was too embarrassed about what was happening and afraid of what Orlando would do if I tried to escape, so I just laid where he left me.

"Who is it?" Orlando asked.

"The front desk." a females voice called out from the other side of the door. Orlando opened the door slightly and looked at the girl. "What's up?" he asked.

The young girl had a concerned look on her face when she asked, "Is everything ok here?"

"Yes, everything is fine." Orlando replied. He could see the girl trying to scan the hotel suite behind him, so he closed the gap in the door with his body so she could only see him.

"We've had some noise complaints about yelling and screaming coming from your room." the girl said.

"Nah. We good. Everything is cool here."

"Ok, well, you're going to want to keep it down because the police have been called and they are on the way here."

"Like I said, there is nothing going on here so if they come, they come."

"Ok, sir, you have a good day."

"You as well."

He closed the door and walked back through the hotel suite to where I was lying. "See, your ass made them call the police. Get up and clean yourself up. I'm out of here." he said.

He grabbed his phone, wallet, and keys and headed to the door. After I heard the hotel door close, I peeled myself off the floor, slowly walked to the bathroom, and looked at myself in the mirror. I felt like I was dying inside. I touched my new bruise and began to cry.

"I can't do this no more." I said.

I thought about packing my stuff and going to my moms, but then I thought about what he said. I wouldn't have anything without him. I would be starting all the way over again. I would go back to a regular life, but without a job or a home. If I got back on my feet, I wouldn't be living in the huge house that I'd become accustom to. I would go back to living in an apartment or condo. I would be giving up my life of luxury, my designer bags and clothes, my VIP status, and the Benz I was driving that Orlando bought me. I asked myself was it all worth it? A question that I had asked myself many times since being married to Orlando. Orlando wasn't the same man he was before we got married. Since being married to him, he was always angry, short patient, and abusive. He didn't compliment me anymore. He barely talked to me, and we were barely making love. It was almost like I was never there unless he needed a punching bag. The days of him being the sweet, attentive, thoughtful guy I met were sparse.

I washed my face, re-applied my make-up, changed clothes, found my pills and took another one. I grabbed my purse and headed out to meet Adara to try my best to enjoy my last day home before heading back to my life away from home as Orlando King's wife.

Chapter 23

Adara

I put my empty wine glass down beside the tub and pulled the plug out of the tub so the bubbly water could drain. I stood up and closed the shower curtains, and then turned on the shower. I put a little more soap on my loofah sponge, rubbed it until it began to lather, and then I washed my body again. The hot water trickling down on my skin helped me relax even more. After dealing with Wes's bullshit at the club, I just needed a moment to myself to get my mind right. I rinsed the soap from my body, and then let the water run over my neck and shoulders for a few more minutes.

My kids were taking a nap and I needed all the me time I could get before linking up with Chanel. It was her last night in town and I wanted to spend as much time as I could with her before she left.

Wes was on his way home to watch the kids while I went out. After I slept on the couch, he promised that he would watch them to make up for not picking them up from my mom like he was supposed to. He apologized numerous times and made a bunch of promises I knew he probably wouldn't keep, but I took him up on his offer just to see if he would keep his word.

I turned the shower off, got out, dried off, and put my robe on. I walked out of the bathroom, into my bedroom, and over to the dresser where I kept my lotion. I heard Wes's keys in the door as I was moisturizing my skin.

He actually showed up. I thought as I heard him close the door and make his way to the bedroom.

"The kids sleep baby?" he asked when he walked into the bedroom.

"Yes." I replied.

He put the keys on the dresser and walked up behind me. He hugged me from behind and said, "Damn you smell good."

"Thank you." I said as I felt him kiss my neck.

"Stop Wes."

"No. It's been a while and I miss my baby."

I rolled my eyes as I felt him kiss my neck down to my shoulders. "I said stop Wes."

"Hush Adara. You know you want this."

He was right. I did. I was in need, but I tried to give him an excuse why I didn't want it.

"Wes, I gotta meet Chanel. She is going to be waiting on me if I don't hurry up and get dressed."

"She'll be fine." Wes said as he turned me around to face him.

He opened my robe, and then he put his mouth on one of my breasts, sucked it, and licked the nipple a few times. Wes kissed his way back up to my lips as his hand found my peach, and then it was over. I couldn't fight it anymore. My head tilted back, and a moan escaped my lips as he rubbed my pearl in circles. As soon as he heard me moan, he picked me up, put me on the dresser, and put his mouth on my peach, He spread my lower lips with his tongue and went to work on my pearl, flicking and sucking on it. I grabbed his head and moaned even louder. I wanted it, so I let him have me. My body needed to release, and Wes was giving me exactly what I needed.

He worked on my peach for a little bit, and then he stopped, stood up, pulled me to the edge of the dresser, and put his tool inside of me. When I felt it, I grabbed on to the edge of the dresser. He did the same while giving me deep thrusts. I wrapped my legs around his waist and rolled my hips into his thrusts. He moaned, and then I moaned. Wes whispered that he loved me in my ear, and I replied the same. He began kissing me while we continued grinding into each other on my dresser, and then his moans got louder. So did mine, and then I screeched when I got my O.

Wes let me feel my orgasm, and then he paused and said, "This pussy good baby."

I griped the edge of the dresser while my body tensed and trembled. Wes felt my walls tighten, so he began to thrust harder until he pulled out to bust into his hand.

He stepped back while trying to catch his breath. I was also trying to catch my breath as I slid off the dresser. Wes smiled, kissed my lips, and then made his way to the bathroom to clean up. I smiled back, watched him walk away, and then I closed my robe back up. I began fixing my hair in the mirror.

Wes returned from the bathroom a few minutes later and said, "Have fun with your friend. I'm going to go check on the kids."

I hurried into the bathroom to clean up from our session, and then I got dressed. He walked me to the door and kissed me goodbye. I got into my car feeling good. Not only did he do what he said he was going to do, but he gave me a good session. It was the first time I had a smile on my face in a long time.

***

I rushed into the restaurant and found Chanel sitting in a booth by herself. She stood up to hug me when she saw me coming. We embraced and then I slid into the booth and said, "Hey sis."

She looked up from her phone and said, "Hey sis. I didn't order anything yet. I was waiting for you and Nikita."

"Ok. Sorry I'm late. I had to get the kids together for Wes to watch them."

"Oh, he's actually watching them tonight?" she asked.

"Girl, yes. He actually kept his word this time." I said.

"Well, good for him. I don't mind that you're late. I just got here myself sis, so it's ok."

I put my purse in the seat next to me, and then I looked across the table at my God sister. Something about Chanel was different. Her energy wasn't the same, and it seemed like she was under the influence of some kind of drug. She was moving and speaking like she was high on something.

Chanel continued to look at her phone and I looked around the restaurant to see if the waitress was around. I wanted to order some water. I was a little parched from the session that I had just had with Wes. It seemed like the restaurant was going through a dinner rush because almost every table in there was full. The waiters looked like they were running around like chickens with their heads cut off. The waitress spotted me searching for her and hurriedly walked over to our table.

"Hi ladies! Welcome. I will be your server tonight. Can I start you off with something to drink?"

"Hello, yes can I get a glass of water with lemon slices."

"Sure, and for you miss?"

"I'll have the same." Chanel said without looking up from her phone.

"Ok. I'll grab those for you and bring you ladies some menus." the waitress said, and then she walked away.

I asked, "Sis, are you ok?"

"Yea, I'm good."

"Are you sure? Seems like you're high or something." I said with a slight chuckle. The waitress came back with our waters and menus and then she walked away to check on another table.

Chanel looked at me and said, "I'm just a little tired sis."

She looked back down at her phone. That's when I saw it. The light from her phone illuminated the bruise under her eye. I could tell that she tried to cover it up with make-up, but I could see it. There were some allegations swirling around in the blogs about possible domestic violence going on in their marriage, but I didn't believe it until that moment.

I put my glass of water down and said, "Hold up. Wait. Look at me."

She looked up from her phone and asked, "What?"

"Is that a bruise under your eye?" I asked.

"Huh? No." she said.

"Yes there is. You have a black eye and you tried to cover it up with make-up."

She shook her head and said, "I don't know what you're talking about sis. I don't have a black eye."

She looked back at her phone, and then I felt myself getting a little angry.

"You're going to sit here and lie Chanel?" I asked, and then the waitress walked back over to our table. I told her that we needed a little more time to look at the menus. She told me she would come back to check on us in a few minutes, and then I looked back at Chanel.

"Is that mutha fucka putting his hands on you?" I asked.

"Nah sis, you're overreacting."

"I'm overreacting? You're sitting here with a black eye and acting like you're on drugs and I'm tripping? Does he got you on drugs too?"

"No." Chanel responded with irritation in voice.

"You're letting him put his hands on you, sis?"

"I said no, so can we stop talking about it?" Chanel responded angrily. She put her phone on the table and looked at me.

"Chanel are you serious? I'm going to kill that mutha fucka. I told you he wasn't no good, but you wanted to go and marry his no-good ass anyways. I can't believe you're covering up his bullshit. For what? Some money? You've got to be kidding me."

Chanel became furious. She frowned at me and said, "Look, why are you coming at me right now? I told you nothing happened. Why can't you just fucking leave it alone. Why are you so worried about me anyways? When you need to be worrying about that dead-beat ass dude you got for a baby's daddy living up in your house rent free not doing shit for you or your kids. You ended it with a doctor for a bum ass dude with no job, no career, and no future. You need to be worried about that and not me, my business, or how my make-up is sitting on my face."

I was completely taken aback by her tone and what she said, I felt myself get angry and I replied, "Oh, you're really fucking tripping and you're disrespectful as hell. All I'm doing is being a concerned friend and you're going in on me like that. You got me messed up Chanel."

Chanel stood up and grabbed her wallet and phone. She said, "I'm going to go because I don't feel like sitting here anymore. I will talk to you another time. Bye."

"Chanel." I said as she was walking away, but she continued walking towards the door without looking back. Nikita walked into the restaurant right after Chanel walked out.

"Girl where is Chanel going? I just saw her storm out of here. She looked mad and she didn't even respond when I spoke to her." she said as she slid into the booth.

I said, "I guess she was mad. She has a black eye."

"What?" Nikita asked.

"Yes. That lame ass dude Orlando is beating on her and she refused to admit it. She's in fucking denial and I think she was on drugs. She was completely covering it up like she was trying to protect him or something."

"Oh my God." Nikita said. "You know what? I knew something was different about her. She just didn't seem like the same Chanel. She was very skinny, and she was really withdrawn and quiet.

"I felt the same way, but I couldn't put my finger on what it was. Now I know, I'm so furious, and I want to beat his ass."

"Me too cousin. I know I don't mess with Chanel like that, but I ain't with the abusive stuff."

"Me either." I exhaled loudly, and then I said, "We're supposed to be meeting Kyra, so let's go."

We stood up and walked out of the restaurant.

Nia Rich

Chapter 24

Adara

We left the restaurant to head to a hair show. It didn't take us exceptionally long to get there. Kyra met us in the parking lot. She had her friend Destiny with her.

"I'm sure y'all remember Destiny."

"Of course. Hi." I said.

Nikita said, "Hey."

She spoke back, and then she asked Nikita, "When are you due?"

"Girl, I'm scheduled to have my C-section next week. I can't wait."

"Well, congrats."

"Thank you."

Kyra asked, "Where is your friend Chanel?"

"Long story girl. I'll have to tell you about it later, but she left."

"Well, let's go before the line gets long."

When we got to the venue, there was already a long line. We walked to the back of the line, a few people entered the line behind us, and then I spotted Leslie: Wes's other baby momma. She was walking up with a friend of hers. They both had colorful hairstyles with matching make-up. I laughed inside about how ridiculous they both looked. *I can't believe that is who he had a baby with.* I thought.

"There go that bitch." Nikita whispered.

"I know. She better not say shit to me." I whispered.

She looked at me, and then she stopped to give her cousin Destiny a hug. After they hugged, she looked at me again, and then she walked to the back of the line. She was about three people behind us, and I could hear her snickering and laughing with her friend, so I knew they were probably talking about me. I knew she was about to get on some petty stuff, and after the argument I had with Chanel, I was not in the mood for more drama.

"I really hope this bitch stays in her lane today." I whispered to Nikita.

"I know because I don't want to have to whoop a bitch ass while I'm pregnant."

"I don't want to have to whoop this bitch ass period." I said.

Leslie couldn't help herself. She started saying petty and antagonizing stuff loud enough for all of us to hear.

"Bitch thinks she's the shit." Leslie said. Her friend starting giggling. "That whack ass hairdo." she said, and then the snickering followed. "Bitch is lame as fuck that's why her man is fucking me."

I knew that I was more mature, and on another level than Leslie, but I'd had enough. I had to say something. I couldn't let her think that I was scared of her or something. She should already know that I can fight from the last time I whooped her tail, but my mother always told me that punks step up to get beat down, so I guess she was ready to catch these hands again.

I turned around and said, "Bitch, if you got something to say to me or about me, you can say it directly to my face instead of behind my back."

Leslie was waiting for me to say something to her, so she immediately snapped back. She yelled, "I do got something to say bitch! You think you're the shit, but you're not. You think Wes is your man, but he's not. He's my man, been my man, and he's at my house every day! Fucking me every night stupid!"

Destiny looked back and yelled, "Cousin stop!" she started making her way to Leslie to try to shut her up.

"I know you a lie bitch because my man is home every night! He will never be yours and that's why you mad! Because you will always be nothing but a side bitch! You will always be fucking and claiming someone else's man! You dumb ass rainbow bright looking ass bitch!" I yelled.

"He fucking me daily and with my kid every day! Why you think he don't answer when you call?! Because he fucking me!" she yelled back. People in the line were listening the verbal altercation but trying not to be involved.

"I don't care! All you are is a side chick, so if he is fucking you, he's still coming home to his family. You the stupid one who had a baby by someone else's man!" I responded.

"Bitch! Fuck you! Leslie snapped. She opened her bottle of water and threw water me.

A few people the line yelled when they felt the water hit their skin. "Aye man! You need to chill!" one guy in the line yelled.

I snapped when the water hit my shirt and I went after her. Kyra grabbed me and pulled me back, and then Destiny grabbed Leslie.

"Delusional bitch!" I yelled as security made their way over to us to intervene.

Kyra said, "No friend, don't let her take you there."

Leslie yelled, "Bitch, I'll beat your ass!"

"You've already tried that and we both know how that turned out!" I yelled. Security walked over to her and asked her to leave.

As they were ushering her away from the venue, she yelled, "Ask Wes who's house he be at when he's pretending to be in the streets! I'll be seeing him tonight! Stupid ass biiitch!"

I apologized to the people standing near me, and then we went inside.

Chapter 25

Kyra

After Leslie and Adara's drama, Kyra just wanted to get home, get into the bath, lie down, and relax because she had to work the next day. Kyra took a relaxing bath, put on her pajamas, and got into bed. No sooner than she closed her eyes, she heard Corey stumbling into the door. She heard him knocking things over as he made his way through the house.

She heard him walk into the room, and then he laid on top of her and slurred, "Baby." she smelled nothing but liquor on his breath. Corey had all his body weight on her, and he felt extremely heavy on top of her. "Babyyyy…" he slurred again.

"What Corey? Get up." she pushed him off her. He slowly fell over to the other side of the bed.

"Why you push me like that Kyra?" he slurred.

"Because you're wasted again Corey." she said as she sat up in the bed.

"No I'm not." Corey slurred. "I'm fine Ky and you always tripping." he said, and the he climbed back on top of her.

"Damn it Corey, I hate when you're like this. You told me that you weren't going to get wasted like this again."

"Shut the fuck up Ky you always running your mouth. Why don't you just shut the fuck up sometimes."

"See, I'm not doing this." she said angrily. She reached over to the nightstand and clicked on the lamp. She pushed him off her again

"Uuuuugh," he groaned when he fell over. "You not doing what? What, you gonna leave me? You always threating to leave me. You're not going anywhere." he slurred.

Kyra stood up and slid into her house shoes.

"Where you going? Come here." Corey slurred.

"Corey you are doing it again."

"Damn why are you getting mad? Doing what?"

"Going down the wrong path again. Coming home wasted like this. You were supposed to be done with this."

"I didn't even have that much to drink." Corey said.

"Whatever Corey."

"Kyra com'ere and give me a kiss."

"No."

"Want to know something?"

"What?"

"I hate that you can't have my baby. I mean never. We will never have baby because you're broken."

Kyra stopped in her tracks, looked at him, and frowned.

"See? I'm not having this fucking conversation Corey. You are so disrespectful." Kyra said, and then she sent a text to Destiny.

Corey is wasted again. I'm coming to your room.

"Where you going, Ky?"

"I'm getting away from you. I told you that I was not going to be dealing with this from you."

"Quit whining so much and loosen up a little."

Kyra put on her pajama pants, her sneakers, and a hoodie.

"Bye." she said.

***

Kyra parked her car in the hotel parking lot and walked into the hotel lobby. Destiny met Kyra in the lobby because the hotel locked the elevator at a certain time and people could only get up to the rooms with a key. They hugged, and then started walking back to the elevators. A black couple came from a different entrance and was walking to the elevators too. They were arm and arm, talking, laughing, and flirting. Looked like they had a good time wherever they were and like they were planning to have a good time once they got to the room. Kyra spotted them, and then stopped dead in her tracks.

"Wait, girl." she whispered and put her hand in front of Destiny.

"What?" Destiny whispered.

"I know that ain't who I think it is." Kyra said.

Destiny looked hard, and then said, "Oh my God. It is."

"Oh my God. Let's back up, so they don't see us."

They backed up behind a large plant and watched the couple through the leaves. They kissed, and then they got on the elevator to go up. The waited until the elevator door closed and then they started walking again.

"Oh my. I don't even know what to say about that." Destiny said.

"Me either. I'm blown away right now, but I had my suspicions."

"What should we do."

"I say, let's just keep it to ourselves right now."

"Good idea."

"That shit is so foul."

"Girl it is."

The ladies got into the elevator lost in their thoughts for a moment.

Destiny asked, "Anyways are you ok?"

"I'm so frustrated. Corey came home wasted again tonight."

Destiny shook her head and put the hotel key the in the door. She asked, "He's just not going to stop, is he?"

"I don't know. It just seems like it's getting worse, and I think he's cheating on me again."

"Why do you say that?" Destiny said as she climbed in the bed.

"Because he is staying out later, and he is getting wasted again. The last time he was cheating on me, he was doing that with her." Kyra said as she climbed in the bed next to her.

"Who Tasi?"

Yup, and I could've sworn I saw a slight hickey on his neck when he was passed out the last time. Girl I never told you that she called his phone and I answered it, but she hung up."

"Ah hell nah girl. That's not ok."

"I asked him if he was sleeping with her again and he said no. He claims he doesn't know why she called.

"Yea right. Whatever he's doing with her isn't right period. Because he might not be fucking her which could be the truth, but that doesn't mean he isn't doing other stuff which is still cheating.

"I already told him, if I find out he is cheating on me, I am done."

"You need to be done, cheating or not. He is not a man. He is a little boy in a man's body. You cannot raise a man bestie."

Kyra paused and let what Destiny said sink in, and then she asked, "You know what he brought up tonight?"

"What?"

"The baby situation."

"Oh wow. He is not right for that."

Kyra teared up and said, "That shit hurts me every time he brings it up. Like it's my fault."

"Right, but you know it's not your fault. You beat cancer."

"Seems like he always brings that up whenever she is in the picture. It's like he blames me for the fact that he has no children yet."

"No. Maybe it's because he keeps getting wasted like he does is the reason that he hasn't had any kids yet."

"He just makes me feel so broken, so less than a woman."

"Girl, there are other ways you can have kids with the right man. Not a little boy pretending to be a man. Don't let him start bringing you down like that. I told you what to do. Get rid of his ass, pack up, and come to Atlanta."

"I hear you bestie. I'm going to bed. Thank you for letting me crash here."

"No problem girl. Good night."

***

The next morning, Destiny was all packed up and ready to head back to Atlanta. Kyra was dressed and ready to leave the hotel to go to work when her phone started ringing. Kyra was putting her last earing in as she answered the phone in her headset.

"Hello."

"Hello is this Kyra?"

"Yes. Who's speaking?"

"This is a nurse from the Hennepin County Medical Center. Your boyfriend Corey Smith was in a car accident last night, well, early this morning and is in stable condition, but we're notifying his emergency contacts."

"Oh my God. Is he ok?"

"Yes, he is ok, will you be coming to the hospital?"

"Yes, yes I'm coming right now. What room is he in?"

"He's in room 1211 down here in Emergency."

"Ok. I'm coming now."

"We'll see you soon."

Kyra hung up the phone and said, "Oh my God. That was the hospital. Corey has been in an accident. I've got to go now."

"Oh no. Do you want me to stay?"

"No. you go home. I'll call you and let you know what I find out." Kyra said as she rushed out of the hotel room.

Chapter 26

Chanel

I was back in New York, back to the huge, luxury home I shared with Orlando, back to my regular life, back to reality. Being there was bittersweet. Part of me was missing my family and friends already. I hated that I got into it with Adara before I left. I wished things weren't the way they were. I wished that I really had the picture perfect life that I tried hard to portray it to be. I wished I had the picture-perfect life I imagined it would be before getting married to Orlando.

I had my suitcase open on the bed and was putting my things away from my trip. Orlando walked in the room, put his suitcase down, and sat on the edge of the bed. He rubbed his bald head, and then he said, "Can I talk to you for a second?"

"For what?" I said solemnly.

"I know your mad at me, but listen to me for a second, please?"

I kept moving and putting stuff away. I really didn't feel like being bothered with Orlando and his shit. I didn't feel like being bothered. I just wanted to have a peaceful day and I didn't know which Orlando I was about to get. I put a couple of shirts in the dresser drawer, closed it, and turned to face Orlando.

Orlando stood up, walked over to me, took both of my hands in his, started crying, and said, "Baby, I'm so sorry for what I did. I know that you're mad at me. I'm mad at myself. I hate that I did what I did. I don't know what is wrong with me. I need to get some help. I just get so mad sometime, and I don't know how to control it. I shouldn't be treating you that way though. You don't deserve that. I love you. It scared me that the hotel called the police. I thought I was going to go to jail. I can't go to jail. I will lose my career and I can't lose my career. I will lose everything I have. I'll lose you. I apologize baby. I do. Please forgive me. I can't lose you. I need you. I will do better. I promise."

I stared into his eyes, watched the tears fall, and then I felt myself starting melt. Something about him felt so genuine. He seemed so vulnerable and broken in that moment. His words felt sincere.

I took a deep breath, exhaled slowly, and then I slowly wiped a few tears from his eyes with my thumb. I said, "Ok. I forgive you. I'm sorry for upsetting you."

"Thank you, baby. It's ok. I'm not worried about that anymore. I'm simply happy that you understand and you're giving me another chance. I can't lose you. I can't lose my career baby. Please help me get some help. Please."

"Ok baby. I will." I said.

He let a few more tears fall from his eyes, and then I let Orlando pull me to him, and I let him kiss me. I didn't stop him when he pushed everything off the bed and laid me down. I let him take my clothes off. I watched him get undressed, and then I let him climb on top of me and make love to me like everything that happened never happened.

Everything felt real for a moment. Everything felt normal for a moment. I felt in love again for a moment.

Only for a moment.

Chapter 27

Adara

After the hair show, I returned home that evening to relieve Wes from his daddy duties. I walked in the house still irritated about my verbal altercation with Wes's other baby momma Leslie. I wanted to beat the breaks off Leslie after she threw the water at me outside of the hair show. After it happened, it was hard for me to calm my nerves. I kept replaying what she said in my head and thinking about how I should've body slammed her. There had been so many times I wanted to put hands on Leslie. Especially after the physical altercation I had with her. That's why I put a restraining order on her to stay away from my shop, but in the back of my mind I knew that I was going to have to face her again, especially after she had a baby by him.

Out of the three other baby's mother's that Wes had, Leslie was the only one I seemed to have a problem with. She never had any reason to hate me. Leslie just hated me because I was in a relationship with Wes, and I had the life that she wanted with him. Also because Wes had whatever he had going on with her that I didn't know about, which according to him, was nothing. To me, it was something and Wes was keeping secrets yet again.

Wesley was sitting on the couch watching T.V. when I walked in the door. He had all the lights off and his feet kicked up on my coffee table. He knows that I hate when he does that. The kids were in their room asleep. He had their door hallway closed so he could hear them. I took my shoes off, set them by the door, and walked over to the Eazy-boy chair next to the couch and sat down.

I said, "Why don't you just sit in this chair so you can kick your feet up? That's why I got it. Instead of putting your crusty feet all on my coffee table."

"Because I can't see the television good from that chair. That's why."

"Well get your feet up off my table." I said.

He moved them and sat up, "Whatever. Did you have fun baby?"

"It was cool." I said.

"Damn I can't get no kiss?"

I looked at him and paused for a moment. I didn't want to kiss him. I really wanted to smack the shit out of him, and he didn't know it.

"What?" he asked.

"Are you still fucking Leslie?" I asked.

He sucked his teeth and said, "Aw come on. That's what you on? Don't start with that bullshit Adara."

"I'm serious."

"Nah man." he responded.

"Don't lie to me." I said sternly.

"I came home like you asked. I watched the kids. I put them to bed, and everything is fine. I'm not trying to talk about or hear nothing about no Leslie."

"I saw her tonight and she was talking big shit about how you still fucking her, you're at her house every day, you're her man, so you're just lying to me? You told me that you don't be over there."

Wes put his head in his hand and began bouncing one of his legs. "That girl be lying. I'm not fucking Leslie."

"Why would she say that then?"

"Because she ignorant like that. Why the hell are you listening to her ignorant ass anyway?"

"Because I don't think that she is lying. She doesn't have any reason to be acting like that if you're not fucking her. She threw water at me tonight."

"She did what?"

"Yea. I almost had to put hands on her again."

"Uuuhhh man."

"So, tell me the truth Wes."

"I already did."

"I don't believe you because we both know that you're good for lying and keeping secrets."

Wes looked at me and snapped. "I ain't got to lie about shit! I already told you I'm not fucking with that girl anymore! The only thing me and her got going on is my baby. Yea, I've been over there a couple of times to see my baby, but she mostly brings my baby to see me at cuz house, so you can get up out my face with that bullshit!"

"Oh, so you *have* been over there?! You never told me that!"

"I didn't think that I had to."

"I'm your woman! I should know if you're up in your dumb ass baby mama's face!"

"I got to see my child Adara."

"You didn't tell me that you were going to her house to do that, so are you fucking her or not?"

"I just told you no! The bitch be lying! She crazy as fuck and she ain't got shit else to do but to make shit up to have you coming home tripping on me!"

I started tearing up. "You're so full of it Wesley! Why would you put me through this again!"

"Man, you tripping. I'm about to go." he said as he stood up and started grabbing his stuff.

I yelled, "Where are you going Wes?! Back over there with her?! Well leave and stay over there since that is where you like to be! You got me over here with two kids and you got the nerve to be lying to me and cheating on me! Fuck you Wesley!"

"I'm not about to argue with you anymore over no stupid shit that crazy bitch said. I told you I'm not fucking with her! I'm not going to say it again!" he said as he was walking towards the door.

I made a mad dash to the door and stepped in front of it. "You're not going anywhere!"

"Move Adara!"

"No! I'm sick of you lying to me!"

"Move Adara!"

"No! I'm not about to let you leave so you can go and cheat on me again!"

"I don't have time for this shit Adara get out of the way!"

"No!"

He picked me up and I just started swinging on him. I know my momma told me to never put my hands on a man, but I was so frustrated that I felt out of control of myself. He took the punches, put me down, and opened the door. I grabbed his shirt, but he yanked out of my grip and walked out the door.

I was mad. I knew that he was lying and there was nothing that I could do about it. Leslie had a child by him too, so she was going to be in his life forever too. I felt so much regret about having another child by Wes. I felt stuck in my situation. I loved him, but he was bad for me. I was mad at myself for loving him, mad at myself for giving the relationship another chance, and mad at myself for having another baby. All my frustration was coming out in that moment.

I closed and locked my door, and then I sat on my couch and cried. After about an hour of crying, my text message notification started chiming. I opened it and read it.

Hey. I hope all is well with you.

It was a text message from Dr. Miles Nash. I blacked out the screen, stood up, and went get into my bed and go to sleep.

**

I woke up the next morning in bed alone. Wes wasn't there. He never came back home. He stayed the night at wherever he ended up the night before. He was probably at Leslie's and I was mad about it, but I didn't feel like calling to find out.

I unlocked my phone to see if he had called or text. Nothing. I tapped on the message Dr. Miles Nash sent to me and read it again. I hadn't responded. I smiled and put my phone on the nightstand. I heard my son crying which meant it was mommy time. It made me feel good that Miles had thought about me after all the time that had passed. I walked in my kids room, picked up my son, and helped my daughter get out of bed, and then I heard my phone ringing. I carried my son back into my room to answer it. It was from an unsaved number. I quickly answered it.

"Hello?"

"This a call from Hennepin County Correctional Facility from Wesley."

I said, "What?" I listened to the automated voice tell me to press zero to accept the charges. I pressed zero, and the call was connected.

"Wesley?"

"Hey baby."

"What are you doing in jail?"

"I got picked up last night after I left the house on some bullshit. They might try to keep me here for a couple of weeks. Call cuz and tell him I'm in here. He'll know what to do."

"Oh my God Wesley."

"I know, but it's going to be ok. Are the kids alright?"

"Yes they are fine."

"Ok good. I love you baby. Don't worry about anything. I'll be home soon. If you need anything Cuz got you. Ok?"

"Ok."

"I got to go, but I will be calling again so make sure you answer this number."

"Ok. love you. Kiss the kids for me."

"Love you too."

I hung up and looked at the phone. I was in shock. How the hell did he end up in jail? *Ugh.* I thought as I laid my son on the bed so I could change his diaper. That news gave me a huge headache. I wasn't sure how I was gonna handle him being locked up or handle my life and my kids while he was locked up. I put the clean diaper on my son, started wrapping up the dirty diaper, and then my phone started ringing again. I answered it quickly.

"Adara?" the woman asked.

"Yes?"

"This is Chanel's mom. She is in the hospital."

I paused what I was doing and asked, "What?"

"She tried to commit suicide last night."

To be continued........

Contact the author

niarichbooks@gmail.com

Nia Rich